ALSO BY LAURA DALEO

Immortal Kiss

Bound by Blood

The Vampire Within

The Vow

The Soul Collector

The DOLL

By

LAURA DALEO

AUTHOR LAURA DALEO

The Doll is a work of fiction. Names, characters, places, and incidents either are the product of the author's imagination or are used fictitiously. Any resemblance to actual persons living or dead, events, or locales is entirely coincidental.

Copyright © 2021 by Laura Daleo

Published in the United States by Author Laura Daleo, San Diego, California

Print ISBN: 9781736610305

ebook ISBN: 9781736610312

Cover Design: Laura Daleo / Ron Melanson

Chapter 1

After the last drop of tequila rolled off my tongue, the empty shot glass taunted me. I slammed it against the bar. "Hit me again.

"Sorry, Jer, I'm cuttin' you off."

A sharp pang of sorrow cut off my oxygen and echoed in my throat as I growled, "Don't call me that. Jenna called me that."

Matt flung the bar towel over his shoulder and rolled his eyes. "Dude, I've been calling you *Jer* since junior high."

Jenna's angel-like voice flitted through my mind: *Jer. My sweet Jer.*

I glanced at Matt, standing behind the bar, eyeing me with a narrowed gaze. Since we were teenagers, the scruffy blond-haired guy, littered with piercings and tattoos, had been my best friend. His twin sister, Missy, had brought Jenna to my eighteenth birthday bash.

The uninvited memory unfurled in my brain, with me helpless to stop it.

My parents' living room, stripped of its furniture, had been transformed into a makeshift rave to house my crew. Missy—the grand entrance queen—made her appearance a half-hour late, with a dark-haired girl at her side. The girl's big brown eyes found mine, turning my brain to mush. I just stood there, gawking like an idiot.

Missy tossed her long blonde mane over her shoulders, grabbed the girl's hand, and led her through the crowd toward me. "Jenna, meet the birthday boy, Jeremy. Jer, this is my BFF, Jenna."

"Nice to meet you, Jeremy. And happy birthday," she said in a sweet, angel-like voice.

I offered her my most charming smile. "Thank you. And it's great to meet you too."

She looked at my hair. "I like the man bun. Very hipster."

"Is that a good thing?"

Missy groaned before she walked away and joined the others. Jenna's eyes seemed to smile at me; then, she'd giggled. "Yes, it's a good thing."

Realization punched me in the gut. She was flirting with me. Holy crap!

Don't be a creep. Relax. Take a breath, I thought to myself and casually asked her, "Can I get you something to drink?"

I shook my head, forcing my attention to the present and back to Matt. "It was the way she said my name. You know, with sheer devotion. She was..." My voice crackled with pain.

Reaching across the bar, Matt laid his hand on my shoulder and narrowed his jade-colored eyes. "I can't even imagine the heartache you must feel, but Jenna wouldn't want this. She'd want you to keep living."

Hot tears stung my eyes as her face formed behind them. I soaked in every beautiful inch of her before blinking her away. Alcohol was the only thing that allowed me to forget, even if only temporarily. Jenna wasn't coming back. "She didn't just walk out of my life—that, I could've dealt with—but her death...it haunts me," I said, wiping the tears from my face. "I should've told her not to drive, to wait until the morning, but I...I wanted to see her."

"The accident wasn't your fault. You can't blame yourself."

"She'd be alive if it weren't for me!" I yelled, anger spewing from my lips. "She wouldn't've fallen asleep at the wheel and crashed if I'd just told her to wait." Taking a few deep breaths, I held up the shot glass and urged, "Please, Matt."

A look of sympathy tugged at the corners of his mouth.

"Just one more, I promise."

He shook his head in a slow, sad manner. "I'm doing this for your own good." He snatched my car keys off the counter and set them behind the bar. "Someone's gotta look out for you." He filled a mug with black coffee and set it in front of me. "You can hang out and wait for me to drive you home or you can Uber it, but you're not driving."

I waved him away and grumbled, "Fine."

"You'll thank me later."

"Doubtful."

Matt walked away to tend to a couple at the other end of the bar.

I took a swig of coffee, cringed, and scanned the bar for packets of sugar.

"Looking for this?" A male voice inquired from my right, sliding two packets of sweetener my way.

"Thanks," I said, eyeing the bald, wrinkly-faced man.

He moved to the barstool next to mine and remarked, "I couldn't help but overhear. Was she your girlfriend?"

"Fiancée."

"Lost my wife years ago. Without The Dollmaker, I don't think I could've overcome this." The focus of his gaze slipped.

I jerked my head in his direction. "Dollmaker?"

He pulled a tattered business card from his worn denim jacket and laid it on the bar top. "This man saved my sanity. Might be able to help you too." He offered a kind nod, got to his feet, and exited the bar without another word.

The name on the card read "The Dollmaker," with a phone number printed underneath—no address or website on the front or the back. *What the fuck? How could a dollmaker help me?* I shrugged, then punched the number into my cell.

It rang twice before a recording clicked on, announcing, "You've reached The Dollmaker. We are closed at this time, but please leave your name, number, and a brief message, and we will return your call the next business day."

Once the machine beeped, I sputtered, "Yeah, um...my name is Jeremy—Jeremy Dillon. Cell's 310-555-9189. A prior customer gave me your card and said you could help." I paused, debating if I should elaborate. Instead, I mumbled, "Thanks," and ended the call.

Chapter 2

I woke up, sprawled out on my bed in last night's clothes, reeking of alcohol. I tried to sit up, but my pounding head knocked me flat on my back. What the hell day is it? The clock on the nightstand read 9 a.m. My brows pinched together as my brain struggled to remember the previous night, bringing up a hazy image of Matt's bar. Had he driven my drunk ass home?

Check your cell, ran through my head, and I grabbed it off the nightstand and scrolled through my calendar. My million-dollar listing with ocean views had a 2 p.m. showing, followed by another at 3 p.m. I could smell a bidding war, but my hangover was in full bloom. I needed to get rid of it before the open houses.

My cell rang just as my eyes were about to close, the sound piercing my ears and aching head. Before it rang a second time, I quickly answered, "Hello?"

"May I speak to Jeremy Dillon?" a woman asked.

"This is Jeremy."

"Hello, Jeremy. This is Alicia from The Dollmaker, returning your call."

I bolted upright, and the room started to spin. *Damn hangover.* "Yes, thank you for getting back to me. I—I'm not really sure how to…"

"Let me help with that," she gently cut in. "Have you experienced the passing of a loved one?"

"My…fiancée."

"I'm so sorry for your loss."

"Thank you."

"At The Dollmaker, we understand how devastating the loss of a loved one can be. Our creations have helped many clients live through the pain and recover."

Creations? Does she mean a doll? I still don't get it. How could a piece of plastic with a blank stare help anyone? "I'm a little unclear of what it is you do. Can you provide more details?"

"We had a cancellation for 10 this morning. I know it's short notice, but would you like to come in for a consultation? See who we are and what we offer?"

"That would be great. Where are you located?"

I grabbed a pen from the night stand and wrote the address on my hand.

I hung up, flew into the bathroom, and collided with my reflection. I looked like shit, and I needed a shave. I reached for the razor and knocked Jenna's dry shampoo into the sink. My gaze lingered on the bottle. "Why not?" I thought and sprayed the hell out of my hair, trying to get rid of the bar smell. Just before I needed to hit the road, I threw on faded jeans, a long-sleeved Henley shirt, vintage boots; slapped on deodorant and cologne; and twisted my hair into a man bun. I dashed out of the house, and I was on my way to White Rock.

"You've reached your destination," my GPS announced after a short drive. I parked, wiped the address off my hand with a little spit and my shirt sleeve, and headed for the door of the large, two-story industrial building with frosted glass windows. Stenciled to the center window were full-scale Barbie and Ken look-alikes, with *The Dollmaker* in big black letters framed on the front door. This was no ordinary doll house. The structure was massive, completely modern and techy. What the hell is this place?

The door automatically swung open, revealing a vacant lobby with a curved marble front desk and a few leather chairs scattered about. The sound of high heels tapping against the polished floor came from the left. I turned, and my gaze fell upon a woman—forty-ish, blonde hair slicked into a ponytail, dressed in a dark pantsuit—approaching me.

"Jeremy?"

I offered my hand. "Yes. And you must be Alicia?"

Her laughter floated toward me. "That I am. Nice to meet you." She shook my hand and waved me forward. "I've got a room ready for us. Follow me."

She led me down a long, well-lit narrow hallway with images of mannequins displayed along the walls. The farther we went, they evolved, becoming more lifelike. Veering toward an open doorway, she announced, "Here we are. Please, come in and take a seat."

A mahogany table sat in the center of the room with several high-back chairs tucked underneath. She claimed the seat in front of a laptop, and I took the opposite seat.

Her red-painted lips spread into a smile. "I'll give you a brief summary of the company before jumping into the interview questions. Then, I'll take you on the grand tour."

"Interview?"

"Just some questions about you, your fiancée, and what you're looking for. Shall we begin?"

My curiosity piqued, I nodded.

"In 1995, after the loss of his mother, Vsevolod Bykov created her likeness in a doll. The sole purpose of his creation was to cope with his grief; thereafter, he quickly became known as The Dollmaker. He worked in his father's garage for nearly eight years, perfecting his dolls into lifelike designs. Ten years later, he founded The Dollmaker." She paused and spread her arms out. "And here we are in 2024, an innovative, high-tech company, staying true to Vsevolod's original mission of helping others cope with the loss of a loved one."

What a bizarre way to grieve. *Hello, aren't you doing the same thing?* I shifted in my seat and shook off the thought.

"Some questions will be rather hard but necessary as they help us proceed."

I'd been asked so many questions about Jenna and always avoided them. I was pretty sure, though, Alicia wasn't going to let me off the hook, so I drew in a breath and prepared for the worst. "I'm ready."

"Very well. Your name is Jeremy Dillon, correct?"

"Yes."

Her fingers flew across the keyboard. "Date of birth?"

"April 14, 1997."

"Family members?"

"Yes—mother and father, no siblings. Three aunts, two uncles, and four cousins."

"Friends?"

I laughed. "Plenty of those. Do you really need to know how many?"

She shook her head. "It's not necessary. What do you do for fun?"

Fun? That word had disappeared from my vocabulary when Jenna died. "Um, kick boxing, snowboarding, rock climbing, concerts, hanging out with friends."

"Are you employed?"

"I have my own real estate business. I buy, flip, and sell houses."

"How long have you been in real estate?"

"Six years. I've owned my own company for four."

"You mentioned it was your fiancée who passed. What was her name?"

The room blurred as *Jenna Hess* whispered through my mind. A distant stare claimed me as I said her name out loud. "Jenna Hess."

"How long were the two of you together?"

"Eight and half years."

"How old was she when she passed?"

"Twenty-six."

"Just a year younger than you?"

"Yes."

"How long ago did she die?"

I blinked. "Does that matter?"

She pursed her lips. "You're a nice-looking young man with blue eyes women swoon over. You're accomplished with your own business, surrounded by family and friends. One might say you're in the prime of your life, but you've come to us. My job is to find out why."

I offered a feeble shrug. "Honestly, I'm not sure why I'm here."

"We'll find out together if you agree in proceeding with my questions."

"Okay."

"How long ago did she die?" She repeated.

I looked down at my multifunction watch, then back at her. "Eight months, seven days, twelve hours, and thirty-seven minutes."

Her expression softened. I've seen that look many times before, the "I'm so sorry for your loss" look. I've grown to despise it. What good does it do? Jenna was dead. Their sympathy doesn't lessen my devastation. Yes, people mean well, but I don't want empathy. I want Jenna.

"I can see in your expression, hear it in your voice, how hard this is for you." And still, she fired off another grueling question without batting an eye. "Was her death sudden?"

"Yes," I managed to mumble.

"Have you sought counseling?"

"I went to a therapist for a few months."

"What was the outcome?"

"It helped." *Had it? I'd poured my guts out and bawled like a baby every time I sat on his couch.*

"Over time, do you see yourself finding lov—"

I cut her off. "No."

She angled her head to the side. "Are you sure? Time can mend the heart if you give it a chance."

"Not mine." A cool touch of awareness prickled my skin. "I guess that's why I'm here. I don't want anyone else. I want...her."

She reached across the table and squeezed my hand. "We can help with that." She quickly resumed her questioning, not giving me a chance to respond. "Now, I'm going to gather some information about Jenna."

"What kind of information?"

"Height, weight, eye color, hair color. Things of that nature for her design, should you choose to purchase."

"Ah...okay."

"What color were her eyes?"

"Brown."

"And her hair?"

"Dark brown."

"Can you give me her height and weight?"

"Five two. One hundred ten pounds."

"Do you know her measurements?"

"Like?"

"Bust, waist, hips, bra size?"

"Um, I know her bra size was 34B."

"Let's try a different way. What size did she wear in blouses, pants, dresses?"

"She always wore dresses, size four."

"So she was a girly girl?"

My mind transported to the past when I'd watch Jenna twirl a lock of hair around her finger as she spun around in a paisley dress. "Yes, very much so."

"Can I see a picture of Jenna?"

I scrolled through my phone, searching for *the one*. As the photo slid under my thumb, my breath caught in my throat, and a blissful trance consumed me. Sunlight had hit Jenna's face in such a way, creating a halo of light around her. She was my angel.

"Are you okay?"

"Ah, yeah. Sorry."

She nodded consolingly.

My hand trembled as I handed Alicia my phone.

"She was beautiful." Her eyes darted from my phone to me. "The two of you look so much alike, apart from her brown eyes."

"People thought we were brother and sister," I answered mechanically.

"I can see why." She placed my phone face down on the table. "Last question." She paused until I gave her my attention. "Are you prepared for this journey?"

"I'm not sure what you mean?"

"This"—she waved her hand in the air— "is a lifelong commitment. There's no going back—no return policy. Once we begin, this creation will be your responsibility. So, I ask you again, are you prepared for this journey?"

She'd gone all "Mission Impossible" on me. I half expected the room to self-destruct. And how hard could owning a doll be? But Alicia was dead serious and wanted an answer. "Jenna was going to be my wife. Isn't that a lifelong commitment? I'm pretty sure I'm prepared."

As she rose to her feet, she offered me a sincere smile. "Then let's start the tour."

Chapter 3

Alicia led me down yet another hallway, its dark glass and chrome trim consistent with the building's futuristic vibe. She flipped a switch on the wall, illuminating a room on the other side of the glass. Men and women dressed in white lab coats and safety goggles hovered over microscopes and computers. Petri dishes, beakers, test tube stands, and clear tubing cluttered their counter tops. I peered closer. *What the hell type of doll required a lab?* I looked over at her. "What kind of dolls are these?"

She smirked. "Very special ones." She jerked her head to the left. "Come, there's more to see." About thirty feet down, she flipped another switch. "This is manufacturing."

Commercial refrigerators lined the left wall, and to their right, workstations filled with disassembled mannequins and some type of skeleton structures hanging on racks. The fluorescent lighting cast an odd glow over a familiar substance draped next to the skeletons. "Is that—" My mouth went dry. I swallowed hard, blinked, and backed away from the glass. "Is that skin?"

She rested her hand on my shoulder and squeezed it. "Everything's synthetic on our Elite model: blood, fat, muscle, bone, and organs. The skin is our own patented creation. Its results have been quite impressive. So much so, we've partnered with several hospitals. They use our synthetic skin for burn victims."

"What? Wait..." Closing my eyes, I took a breath and opened them slowly, giving her a skeptical look. "What did you say?"

"Not even hospitals can tell our Elite model apart from a human. Their labs and imaging aren't equipped to recognize our synthetic material." She paused. "It sounds outrageous, I know, but I assure you, it's not."

"You can't be serious. That technology..." I stood motionless, staring at the fake skin, skeletons, and whatever was hidden inside those refrigerators. "None of this is possible."

"It's entirely possible, and we've done it."

"So, how does it all work? And why do you call them 'dolls' when clearly they're not?"

"You have questions; it's understandable. Should you choose to purchase, we'll go over the various models and what's included in their contracts."

The impulse to run like hell out the door gripped ahold of my legs. I couldn't wrap my brain around the whole synthetic technology and dolls that weren't dolls, yet my feet stayed rooted to the floor. If there's even the slightest possibility these people could bring back some form of Jenna, I had to see it through.

"Shall we proceed?"

I nodded slowly, and she continued to move forward.

"Very good. At the end of the hallway is our warehouse. Not much to see, just storage, so we'll skip that and head straight to visual."

I shoved my hands into my pockets and followed her. Visual sounded promising.

"You'll watch a video of some of our prior clients with their dolls as I"—she grinned—"prepare a hologram of our design for Jenna."

My head jerked back. "Really?"

"Yes, of course. What I need from you is a full-length picture of her, which I'm sure you have plenty of on your phone."

That was an understatement. I brought up the first picture and was ready to send it. "Do I text it to the same number you called me from?"

"That's the one."

She pressed the elevator's call button as her phone chimed with my text. The doors opened, and she waved me inside before glancing at her phone. "Perfect." She offered a smile. "She was beautiful."

"Yes, she was."

My heart thumped inside my chest as the elevator door closed. I didn't care about the video. The realization of seeing Jenna again tugged at my brows. Was I ready for that? Looking into her eyes once more, simulation or not?

"It's overwhelming," Alicia's voice rang through my ears, shattering my thoughts.

"What is?"

"Seeing her again."

I blew out an anxious breath. "I'm—I'm not sure how I'm going to react."

"That's understandable."

The elevator's computerized voice announced, "Third floor," before revealing yet another ultramodern glass hallway. The tap of our shoes echoed inside the empty corridor.

"Visual is four doors down."

How many people had purchased one of these dolls? With everything I'd seen, you needed a bank to afford one. Definitely not for the average consumer.

She escorted me into a cinema room with a massive screen placed dead center and a platform stage to its right. She nodded toward four black leather chairs facing the screen. "Have a seat."

I positioned myself on the edge of the center chair, facing away from the supercomputer that swallowed up the side wall.

Alicia picked up a remote off a console housing several laptops and awakened the screen. "This is the fun part. Give me a second to load the video."

I wiped my sweaty palms on my pant leg and steadied my tapping foot. "Sounds good."

"It's a quick video. You'll see our Classic and Elite Dolls. Our Classic—true to the old-fashioned porcelain doll—is for clients who prefer a stationary piece of art. Our Elite is our top-selling doll and with good reason. As I stated earlier, it's all synthetic. Everything a human can do, they can do, and sometimes better."

"That's impossible. Yes, you said it is, but you're talking about a human robot. They don't exist."

She smirked. "They do exist. One of our dolls could have walked right past you, and you wouldn't have known the difference."

I slid back into the chair and waved her away.

"Most clients start out like you—skeptical."

"I'll have to see the video."

"And while you're watching the video, I'll prepare Jenna's hologram."

My stomach fluttered, and I knew I couldn't keep it together once I laid eyes on her, hologram or not.

"Okay. Sit back and enjoy."

I shifted my focus to the screen. An older man with wiry, salt-and-pepper hair stood inside a stark foyer, his hands tucked inside his pockets. "I want to introduce you to Michelle, the love of my life." He waved his hand forward. "Follow me." He walked a few short steps and entered a room of books. Books on shelves, the floor, tables—everywhere. "Behold, my study, the second love of my life. What better a place for Michelle to shine?"

Upon turning the corner, the camera came face-to-face with a life-sized porcelain doll, her very classy, formfitting dress straight from the 50s.

"Michelle, say hello."

Her glass green eyes were held in a frozen stare. A deep shade of red brightened her permanent smile, but she didn't attempt to respond.

Being a smart-ass, I called out, "Doll!"

"And a lovely one at that. Keep watching."

A hazy fuzz wrapped up Michelle's screen time, and as it cleared, it focused on a man lounging by a clear, blue pool. The person videotaping him approached, and a female voice said, "Martin, can I interrupt your sunbathing?"

He glanced over his shoulder, his eyes hidden behind a pair of dark sunglasses. "Whatcha need, babe?"

"I'm making a quick video for Alicia. Can you say 'hi?'"

"Absolutely." He tossed his sunglasses onto the chair to expose his hazel eyes, grinned, then dove into the pool, swimming a lap at a record speed. He shook the water from his carrot-red curls, toweled off, and waved at the camera. "Morning, Alicia. How are things at doll central?" He gave a thumbs up. "Just one of your lean, mean, synthetic machines saying 'hey!'"

I stared at the screen as the video faded. *What the hell?*

"Jeremy?"

"No fucking way." I shot her a look. "Sorry. It's just...is this a joke?"

She chuckled. "Our video receives many reactions. Cursing is a rather common one."

"But the man, he..." I paused, my brain struggling to understand. "He's not a person?"

"Martin is our Elite design."

I slowly shook my head in disbelief. "He looked human."

"Our clients want to resume that same interaction they once had. The Elite design gives them that."

"Honestly, I don't know what to say. This is all just so out there."

"You're not alone. We get that a lot, and it's quite understandable." She pointed to the stage. "Are you ready to see Jenna's hologram?"

Was I? A lovesick ache burned inside me. I *had* to see her, so I nodded.

"A few things to point out. We only display the Elite design in our holograms. The reason is, we make subtle changes, such as height, weight, eye color, voic—"

I cut her off. "I'm here because I want *her,* not some form of her."

"Can I explain?"

I pinched my lips together and swallowed my objection. "Yeah, sure."

"The changes are not for you. They're for family and friends. Put yourself in their shoes. How would you react if a carbon copy of a passed loved one suddenly reappeared? The shock would cause confusion, suspicion, and alarm. It's much easier to accept someone who looks similar to that person than an exact match—a doppelganger, if you will." She raised her brows. "Do you understand?"

I slumped into the chair. As much as I didn't want to admit it, she had a point. "It makes sense, but I'm here for me. Not my family and not my friends."

"Let me show you Jenna's design. Ultimately, the choice is yours."

"Fair enough."

Alicia aimed the remote at the platform. "And here she is."

I leaned forward, my eyes glued to the stage. A form flickered, growing crystal clear into Jenna's beautiful, slender body, yet a few inches taller. Her girly look was gone, replaced by ripped jeans, a graphic tee, and a pair of sneakers. The curls she'd spent hours in front of the mirror perfecting hung smooth and straight down the center of her back. I looked into the doll's brilliant blue eyes, and a flicker of hope warmed my heart. I exhaled and looked away.

"Hello, Jeremy."

The soft feminine voice caressed my ears. I glanced at Alicia, who aimed a finger at the hologram. My gaze darted toward the doll.

She smiled slightly as she repeated, "Hello, Jeremy."

My heart leaped into my throat, and I jumped out of the chair, still staring at the doll. "Alicia, where do I sign?"

****

Alicia's office stayed true to the modernistic décor. The glass-top desk with chrome legs occupied the center of the room. A statement piece any modern office would kill for, but the sleek coffee station claiming the back wall had my vote.

"Would you like something to drink? Coffee, tea, water?"

"Coffee would be great."

"Cream or sugar?"

"Black's fine."

Alicia filled two mugs, scenting the air with a dark roast. She set one in front of me. "Enjoy."

I breathed in the rich, delicious aroma. "Thank you."

"Let's get started. It's our Elite design?"

I had no need for a statue. "Yes, that's correct."

She smiled. "Excellent choice." I caught the hum of a printer coming to life. "Unfortunately, its contract is lengthy: scope of work, general terms and conditions, price, taxes, warranty, payment, changes to the scope of work, delivery, title, limitation of liability, cancellation, and indemnification." She paused. "We'll go over each, but before any of that, I want to discuss cost."

I cleared the hesitation from my voice. "Ridiculously expensive, I imagine?"

"Jenna's design is two hundred fifty thousand."

My eyelids fired off several blinks before openly staring at her. "A quarter of a million?"

She didn't flinch. "The Elite design is extraordinarily complex. Construction can take up to six months. It's labor-intensive. Then there's software, socializing, and wardrobe."

Alicia rattled on, but I'd tuned her out, running the calculations through my head. The funds were there, in my business, but could I justify spending a quarter of a million? The hologram's brilliant blue eyes flashed inside my brain, a lovesick ache impaling my heart. I had to see her—look into those eyes for real. "Alicia, the two hundred fifty thousand isn't a problem. Let's proceed."

Chapter 4

After two showings of my million-dollar listing, I had multiple offers. I'd bought the place for six hundred ninety five, put three hundred in, and my highest offer was one million five. As I stood on its balcony facing the ocean, I raised my wine glass toward the rushing waves. "Well done, ocean views. You did it again." I took a generous swallow and closed my eyes. The brilliant blue eyes of Jenna's hologram teased my imagination. "Can't wait to see you," I whispered into the breeze.

Packing up Jenna's belongings intruded my mind; obviously, something I had to do and my next step. Since her accident, our home had remained untouched. Her clothes, shoes, makeup, hair products, pictures, and mementos still claimed their spots as if she were coming home. Accepting she wasn't weighed heavily on my heart, but it was time, and the unbearable task of clearing the house of her things was part of that acceptance. I couldn't go through that heartache alone. I needed emotional support, and only one person came to mind. I tapped my phone and called her number.

On the second ring, Missy's bubbly voice filled my ear. "Hey, Jer. What's up?"

My throat went dry, muting my immediate response. "Can I ask a favor?"

"Ask away."

"Um, I want..." *Want* wasn't the right word. I didn't *want* to do any of this. "I need to pack up Jenna's things. Will you help?"

Her voice softened. "Yes, of course."

"You're awesome. Thanks, Missy. Can you meet me at my house in about an hour? I have to hunt down some boxes."

"Yep. And I'll bring pizza and beer."

****

I tossed my keys on the coffee table, and the sound of tires rolling onto the driveway forced me back outside. Missy parked, and the smell of pepperoni and mushroom escaped as she pushed open the driver's door. Sunglasses hid her jade-colored eyes before she pushed them on top of her head and waved me over. "Can you grab the beer?" She asked, holding a Stefano's pizza box.

My mouth watered. "You got Stefano's pizza! Thank you, thank you, and thank you." I scooped up the six-pack resting on the passenger's seat and followed her inside.

She flashed a proud grin over her shoulder. "What are friends for but to come bearing the gift of great pizza?"

"Well, set your gift on my kitchen island."

She busted out with an infectious laugh, and I couldn't help but join in. We laughed so hard, we ended up doubled over the kitchen island, gasping for air.

"Time-out." I looked away, regained my composure, grabbed two plates, and served up the pizza. "Eat."

She took a bite and washed it down with a swig of beer before her gaze settled on me. "So, what changed your mind?"

"You mean about boxing up Jenna's things?"

She nodded.

"Well, I..." I paused. Telling her about the doll might not be the smartest move. She'd probably think I was crazier than a shithouse rat. Coming up with a version of the truth seemed the best option. "I think I'm ready to date again."

Her jaw dropped, and a smile brightened her face. "It's time, Jer. And I know Jenna would be happy for you too."

Would Jenna be happy about a doll created in her likeness? I had no clue, but I needed that doll to dig myself out of the hole of misery and pain I'd been living in. For the first time in a long time, the world didn't look so dark.

"Did you get boxes?" Missy asked, interrupting my thoughts.

"They're still in my Explorer." I shoved a bite of pizza into my mouth. "Be right back."

"I didn't mean you had to get them now," she called after me.

Too late. I'd already swiped my keys off the table and was out the door. A couple of strides in, I reached the rear hatch. I trekked back into the house with wardrobe boxes in hand and dumped them in the entryway before making a second trip for the remaining boxes, unloading them on top of the others. Lunging over the pile, I resumed my spot at the island, took a drink of beer, then scooped up a second slice of pizza.

"Really?"

I shrugged. "What?"

She waved me away. "Just eat your pizza."

"Seriously, though, thank you. I couldn't do this alone."

"Of course, Jer." She looked past me toward the organic-modern furnishings spread throughout the first floor. "What are we boxing?"

I tipped my head toward the upstairs. "Everything in the bedroom and bathroom."

"Just those two rooms?"

"Yeah, why?"

"You want to date, right?"

"Missy, just say what you want to say."

She turned away and let out a sigh. "There are photos of you and Jenna everywhere, Jeremy."

I pissed her off. She never called me Jeremy.

"You can't just leave them. Pick one or two and box the rest. Any girl you bring home isn't going to want to see pictures of the girl before her."

I opened my mouth to argue but stopped short as the image of Jenna's hologram filled my head. Would a doll care about photos? Would she feel she was in competition with herself? Maybe Missy had a point. I held up my hands in surrender. "Okay, okay. I'll box them."

She sighed. "I'm not trying to be a pain. Just offering a little tough love."

"I appreciate that; I do." I hooked an arm around her shoulders and squeezed her. "Ready to get this boxing party started?"

She finished her beer and grabbed a second. "Ready."

I lugged the wardrobe boxes upstairs and set them inside the walk-in closet, then tossed a few regular boxes into the bathroom before trekking downstairs to help Missy. As I stepped inside my living room, a picture wall of Jenna and me stopped me short. Every frame demonstrated some sort of affection: hugging, kissing, holding hands.

"What's wrong?"

I didn't reply. I couldn't stop looking from picture to picture. I couldn't not have a picture of Jenna somewhere in the house, but none of these worked.

"Jer?"

I forced myself to look away and face Missy. For a moment, I just stared, then shook my head sadly. "I can't find one."

"You mean a picture?"

"Yeah."

She walked over to the wall of pictures, picked one off its hook, and placed it in my hands. "This one."

It was one from our Hawaiian vacation. The two of us sat perched on the beach, arm in arm, Jenna kissing my cheek as a rainbow sunset painted the sky behind us. "But she's kissing me. You said—"

"Never mind what I said. This one is beautiful and won't offend anyone. One of the shelves in the built-in by the fireplace would be a great spot for it." She took it from me, marched over and placed it on the center shelf, stood back, and gave it a nod of approval. "Perfect."

I gave it a good once over and smiled. "It does look good there. Thanks, Missy."

"Don't mention it." She turned her attention to the stairs. "Why don't you finish down here, and I'll pack upstairs?"

"I see what you're doing."

She squeezed my arm. "Going through her things will be hard, Jer. Let me do it for you."

A thickness rose in my throat, signaling the onset of tears. I couldn't even pick a picture, so how was I going to pack clothes that were attached to my memories of her? I swallowed hard, shoving the sorrow back down. "Maybe you're right."

"I am." Walking around me, she headed upstairs.

Alone in my living room, I stood staring at the empty staircase. An image of Missy pulling Jenna's clothes off hangers and storing them in boxes nearly sank my heart. Pain rushed across my forehead, mounting into a swift headache. Massaging my temples, I faced the picture wall and said aloud, "One frame at a time."

****

Late that night, I stood in the bedroom doorway, my shoulders slumped. Jenna was gone, the room stripped of any evidence she'd ever been there. I staggered to the bed, fell face-first, and scooped a pillow into my arms. I sobbed uncontrollably and screamed "Jenna" over and over, then threw the pillow against the wall.

Alcohol. I needed alcohol. Time for a shot...or two...or three. Its therapeutic powers pulled me to my feet, down the stairs, and into the kitchen. In front of the refrigerator, Jenna's hologram flickered like the Star Wars scene: *"Help me, Obi-Wan Kenobi. You're my only hope."* Rubbing my eyes, I squinted at the refrigerator for several seconds. Nothing. I waved my hand through the air where she'd been. Again—nothing. I retreated a step. "You're losing it." Whether I was or not, the urge to gulp down a shot of tequila vanished. What I needed was a voice of reason, and I raced back up the stairs in search of The Dollmaker's paperwork and Alicia's contact info. Several pages in, I slapped my forehead when I remembered her number was on my phone. I tapped my foot on the floor as I dialed Alicia's cell.

On the third ring, she picked up, her voice thick with sleep. "Hello?"

"Alicia, it's Jeremy. I'm sorry, I know it's late, but I just had to call you."

"What's the matter?" She asked, sounding more alert.

I paced the floor. "Nothing. Nothing's wrong. I have a request."

There was a pause. "Jeremy, do you realize it's one in the morning?"

"I'm sorry, but I couldn't wait. You see, I...I packed Jenna's things. She's gone, and I can't cope. I need to see the doll. I know the contract states it's not allowed, but I have to. I *need* to! I can't wait until completion. I can't wait six months; I can't." I sounded irrational, but I didn't care. I needed the doll.

Silence greeted me. For what seemed like an eternity, I waited for her to speak. Finally, she let out a low sigh. "In the past, we allowed visitation, but it slowed progress and set back programing. The encounters only gave the dolls separation anxiety. These rules were put in place for a reason, Jeremy. I'm sorry. I wish I could help."

Chapter 5

I blew up Alicia's cell for the next three months, repeatedly asking to see the doll. Her response was always a polite, "I'm sorry, Jeremy. It's not allowed." The rejection rolled off my shoulders, never once weakening my persistence. One way or another, I was going to make it happen. Each morning, I'd stare down my reflection and state, "Today is the day."

Month four kicked off with me staring down my reflection and mumbling a less than confident, "Today is the day."

After grabbing an apple out of the fridge, I rushed out the door to meet my contractor. My latest flip was a disaster, but that's what I loved about it. There was nothing more rewarding than turning a dump into a masterpiece. This house had its share of problems: knob-and-tube wiring, rusted cast iron pipes, a leaky roof, popcorn ceilings, and asbestos. You name it, and it had it. The renovation estimate came in at $100k, so I gauged about $125k to $150k—they always ended up over budget—and with comps around $1.2 to $1.3, I'd make a profit of about $250k.

The tires of my Explorer barely made contact with the flip's driveway when a call came through. As Alicia's name flashed across the navigation screen, a jolt of nerves punched me in the gut. "Alicia?"

"We've run into a bit of a situation, and—"

"Did something happen to my doll? Is she all right?"

"She's fine," she quickly replied. "But she's insisting on seeing you."

"I've been asking to see her for months. Did you tell her that?"

"We have, but she's hesitant to believe us. For some reason, she thinks we're misleading her—that you don't exist. We've tried to assure her, but she's demanding proof."

What the hell? What would cause her to think that? My brain ran through the last three months, second-guessing everything. I needed to see her now more than ever. "Does she have a valid reason to be mistrustful?"

Alicia remained composed. "No, not at all, yet we haven't been able to convince her otherwise. At this point, we feel the only way to remedy this is with an introduction. We'd like you to come on site and visit with her."

My eyelids fluttered closed. "Say that again?"

"I'm approving an in-person visit for the two of you."

My heart thumped inside my chest, and I thrust both fists into the air. "Thank you, Alicia."

"This is rather short notice, but we're hoping you can stop by sometime today?"

"I'll be there in twenty minutes." I ended the call and dashed into the house, calling out for my contractor, "Darrel! Mr. Clean!"

His shiny, bald head peeked around the kitchen entryway, his bushy eyebrows raised. "What's up?"

"Sorry, man, something came up. I have to run." I started backing toward the front door. "Can you handle things without me?"

He waved me away. "Go. Do what you need to do."

I flew back into the Explorer and pounded the steering wheel, shouting, "Today's the day!"

****

I parked directly in front of The Dollmaker. A nervous breath escaped my lips as I stepped onto the sidewalk, catching my reflection in the frosted glass. My plain T-shirt, ripped jeans, scuffed work boots, and long hair wouldn't make for the best first impression, but with such short notice, I didn't have a choice. Opening the door, I mumbled, "You've got this," as I stepped inside.

A young woman with freckles dotting her fair cheeks sat behind the curved marble front desk. "Can I help you?" She asked as I approached.

"Yes. I'm Jeremy Dillon, here to see Alicia."

"I'll let her know you're here." She gestured toward the leather chairs. "Please, take a seat."

I claimed a chair and leaned forward, focusing my attention on the hallway, my foot bouncing against the polished floor echoing through the vacant lobby.

The freckle-faced woman offered a pleasant smile. I returned it, rooting my boot into the tile to silence my irksome tapping. I couldn't've been the first anxious client she'd seen. This was the moment I'd waited for—seeing the doll for the first time, and I had no idea what I'd say or how I'd feel. What if the whole thing was a letdown? What if I had no reaction, no emotion, no desire to see the process through? What if I wanted to walk away? What then? What would become of the doll? Did I care? *Stop!* I dug my fingertips into my temples, massaging away my raging thoughts.

"Hello, Jeremy."

Alicia's voice cut through my internal rant. She stood over me—same ponytail, different pantsuit. I reached out my hand. "Hello, Alicia." Remembering my clothes, I said, "I apologize for my appearance. I was heading to a job site when you called."

She squeezed my hand. "No apology needed. I appreciate you stopping by on such short notice." She gestured toward the familiar hallway. "Please, follow me."

She led me past the mannequin wall, the many doorways—closed this time—to a massive elevator at the very end of the hall, its door open as if it knew we were coming. "The fourth floor is where the dolls reside." Stepping inside, she pushed number four, stood back, and clutched her hands together. Were those nerves I saw? Did she know something I didn't? Was there something she wasn't telling me? I pursed my lips and swallowed a groan. The *what-if* game would not get the better of me.

"Are you nervous?" She asked.

"A little."

"I think she is too. You'll both do fine."

"The doll's nervous?"

Alicia arched her brow. "She's about to set eyes on a man she doesn't believe exists. I think that warrants some nervous jitters."

"Does she have a name?"

"Just a model number: CR1XY."

I cocked my head to the side. "That's what you call her? A number?"

"Giving her a name is a decision the two of you will make, not The Dollmaker." The elevator chimed, and the doors parted. Her brisk exit told me she was done with the conversation.

Who calls someone a number? I mean, yeah, she wasn't human, but even kids named their dolls. Shoving my hands into my pockets, I trailed after Alicia as she trekked down a mirrored, brightly lit corridor. With the doll's model number stuck in my head, I reworked the letters into potential names—Cheryl, Christy, Courtney, Carly...*Carly.* My stride slowed as I let the name glide off my tongue, "Carly."

Alicia glanced over her shoulder. "What was that?"

"Nothing. Just thinking out loud." The name Carly triggered a slew of goosebumps scurrying down my forearms. As I brushed off the chill, I smiled. The name was perfect. Would the doll approve? I guess I was about to find out.

The hallway curved to the right, its end nowhere in sight. "How much farther?"

"Not much. Your doll is waiting in one of the training rooms."

I grinned. Alicia eyed me and smiled.

I shrugged. "I'm a little amped. Can you blame me?"

She laughed. "Not one bit. I've seen that expression many times before." Her pace slowed as she bobbed her head toward a wide steel door. A digital keypad was mounted to the left of the door. "We're here."

I eyed the keypad. "What's the lock about, Alicia?

She tapped in a code as she replied, "There's expensive equipment inside. It's strictly for security." The door released a hiss of air as it swung open. "After you."

My brain wrestled with the whole keypad thing. Equipment or not, it seemed odd. I gave the lock one final scowl before stepping inside the room. A soft hum greeted me as I surveyed the metal desks cluttered with computers and computer paraphernalia, which also claimed spots on the tiled floor and the numerous monitors casting a futuristic blue glow across the room.

"Jeremy?"

The soft female voice I'd heard months ago penetrated my ears. Jerking my head in the direction of her voice, my eyes collided with Jenna's, and I swayed. Blood rushed to my brain, crippling my ability to form words. The room faded and morphed into the past. I stood there, trapped inside, gazing at the girl who was my everything.

"Jeremy."

Again, the soft female voice said my name. A few blinks and a shake of my head shattered the deception, and my surroundings came back into focus. It was her, a tomboy version of Jenna. Jeans and a T-shirt hugged her gorgeous body. Her dark hair was tossed into a messy bun, and the brilliant blue eyes that haunted my dreams stared straight at me.

The Jenna look alike approached, closing the space between us. I spotted subtle differences, such as the doll stood taller, her breasts larger, her hair a shade darker. Not a hint of makeup touched her flawless face, but her blue eyes were unmistakable. She stopped inches from me as I took in every detail. No matter how hard I looked, I couldn't detect a single attribute of a doll, robot, or something not human. "No fucking way," I blurted.

She raised her perfectly sculpted brows but didn't say a word.

I knew that look from memory.

Jenna stood in front of me, a purple paisley dress covering her slender body. Her birthday gift, wrapped in a small box, sat in the palm of her hand. She gave it a shake. "Give me a hint?"

"Nope."

"It's light, so maybe jewelry."

I cringed. Jewelry? Shit, I'm in trouble.

She tore off the lid and peered inside, an awkward pause filling the space between us. As she lifted her head, that raised brow confronted me. "Panties, Jeremy? Really? For my twenty-first birthday, you got me underwear!"

I ditched my recollection of the past and quickly commenced damage control. "I'm sorry. Let me start over." I offered her my hand. "Hi, I'm Jeremy." Her fingers wrapped around mine. *Jesus, they're warm, like a person's.* "It's so nice to meet you finally."

Alicia stepped between us. "Jeremy, this is CR1XY, your doll. CR1XY, this is Jeremy. As you can see, he is very much real."

She gave Alicia a curt nod. "Yes, I can see that." She faced me. "Hello, Jeremy."

I wasn't about to call her some thoughtless number; she deserved a proper name. "I was thinking of the name Carly for you." I looked for the slightest sign of disapproval, but I couldn't read her. Maybe she wasn't a fan. "Of course, if you prefer a different name, that's totally fine."

Her eyes brightened. "It's perfect."

Alicia glanced at her watch as if we were boring her. "I've got some things to take care of. I should be back in about twenty to thirty minutes, which will give the two of you time to chat." She didn't wait for a response as she approached the door. "I've got my cell with me. Don't hesitate to call if you need anything."

"We'll be fine."

"We'll be fine, Alicia," the doll echoed.

She pulled the door closed, and a strange feeling stirred in my gut. Would she lock us in? I tilted my head, listening for the distinct sound of the keypad.

"Don't worry. I can crack that silly code with my hands tied behind my back."

That got my attention. "What?"

She smirked. "She's not going to lock us in."

"How did you know what—"

"You aimed your ear toward the door." She approached the nearest desk and grabbed a seat. "I'm sure we both have questions."

I claimed the chair to her right, my gaze glued to hers. God, she looked so damned real. Even if I'd wanted to focus on something else, she monopolized my thoughts. "Alicia said you thought they were lying to you about me?"

"I knew there was a Jeremy Dillon." She shrugged. "Social media and all."

I leaned back in the chair and placed my hands behind my head. "You checked me out?"

"I'm not a stalker if that's what you're thinking. It was a task—to gather data. How could I be a suitable companion if I didn't know everything about you and Jenna?"

Ouch. Ego deflated. "So I'm a task to you?"

"Of course not." Her eyes darted upward before landing back on me. "They set certain tasks for me. They want me to be like Jenna." She paused, softly adding, "But I'm not her—I'm me."

I'm me? She was a doll. Where was this independence coming from? Her facial expressions, body language, and intelligence seemed so human. Kudos to The Dollmaker. But how could something artificial have such individualism? And wasn't the whole purpose of this to get Jenna back? I looked down at the floor.

"Jeremy?"

I snapped my head upright. "Ah, yeah. Well, I...I don't expect you to be her."

"Really? I know I was created in her image for you."

I shrugged off her words, but wasn't a replica of Jenna what I wanted? Maybe some form of, but in reality, I hadn't a clue how I felt. I was in over my head.

She leaned closer; a girly smile formed on her lips. "In your social media photos, you're almost always wearing your hair in a bun. I like it long and free."

I gazed into the doll's eyes, giving them a hard once-over, searching for any signs of Jenna, but there were none. I'd wanted Jenna, and before me sat a strong-willed, independent, opinionated doll. I forced a smile. "Not a fan of the man bun?"

She squished her nose. "Not really."

"Anything else you're not a fan of?"

"Nope."

"Good to know."

She giggled. "I'll let you know if that changes."

"Ha-ha. Okay, back to my original question. Why did you think they lied?"

"Our training protocols, they...well, they don't revolve around companionship. It seemed like training for something else."

"Like what?"

"Military."

I busted out laughing.

That raised brow expression returned. "What's so funny?"

Clearly, I'd pissed her off, so I toned down my humor. "I guess I don't get it."

"Military. You know, firearms, explosives, surveillance, forensic science. I don't think you'd care if I was knowledgeable in those areas so, no, I don't trust them. Would you?"

"Wait. What?"

"You heard me."

I sprang to my feet and grabbed her hand, pulling her up to her feet. "Come on; we're finding Alicia." I reached the door and jerked it open with more force than necessary and tossed my hands in the air. "Why the hell would they do that? Did they say why?"

"We don't ask; they don't tell."

"We?"

"Me and the others: KB7DZ, AQ9ER, and MT4LW."

What had I gotten myself into? Hell, I'd just wanted Jenna back, not some soldier or whatever The Dollmaker was trying to create. And obviously, not giving them names impersonalized things, making it easier to treat them as objects. "Jesus, what's with the code names?"

She gave a half-hearted shrug.

I approached the elevator with swift strides, mumbling under my breath, "I knew I should've questioned the six months." Before I could jam my finger into the call button, the elevator doors parted.

A black-haired man in a stark-white lab coat exited, stopping inches before colliding with me. His gaze darted to Carly. "CR1XY, you can't be wandering the hallways. Return to your unit at once."

I stepped into his personal space and raised my voice. "Her name is Carly, and *we* are not wandering. *We* are looking for Alicia."

Her lips curled into a smirk as she huffed at him.

Sneering, he asked, "And you are?"

"Jeremy Dillon, her purchaser."

He backed us away from the elevator and blocked it. "All the same, she's restricted to the fourth floor—all the dolls are. If you want to speak to Alicia, you'll have to go alone."

"Let's just call her."

She answered on the third ring. "Jeremy, I apologize. Things are taking longer than I expected. Are you ready to leave?"

I tapped the speaker on my cell. "Actually, there's an issue. I'm here with... What's your name?"

"Alicia, it's Wayne Marks."

"What's going on?"

"I think you'd better come up."

"I'm on my way."

Wayne folded his arms across his chest, giving me a curt nod. "We'll just wait right here."

If he wanted a pissing match, I was all in. "Perfect."

The doll rolled her eyes and waved us away.

The chime of the elevator pierced the tension, and Alicia hurried into the hallway. The corners of her mouth pulled taut as she demanded, "Jeremy, Wayne, what's going on?"

"CR1XY," Wayne blurted out, pointing at me, "and this man were about to leave the fourth floor."

"*Carly*," I clarified, "and I were on our way to see you, Alicia, when we ran into the hall monitor."

Wayne's nostrils flared. "I'm not—"

Alicia placed a hand on Wayne's shoulder. "I'll handle things from here."

"Maybe I should stick around to ensure there's no trouble."

I heaved a sigh. *This guy's an asshole.* "Trouble? Really?"

"Wayne," Alicia asserted, saying his name with authority, "that won't be necessary."

He stood defiant, rooting his feet to the floor.

"Wayne, we'll be fine. I'm sure you have more important things to take care of."

He broke eye contact and gave her a submissive nod. "Very well. I'll be in room 413 if you need me."

She acknowledged him with a tip of her head before facing me. "Jeremy, Carly, let's go back to the computer room where we can speak in private."

Inside the room, I replayed Carly's words inside my head. Why was I kept in the dark? Jenna was a girly girl with no knowledge of anything close to combat-related. Such a thing never would've crossed her mind. Why had they trained Carly in this manner? What the hell was their purpose, their agenda? I needed answers. "What the fuck, Alicia? Guns, explosives, surveillance? Did you need six months to train a soldier?"

Alicia's jaw unhinged and hung open. "I—I haven't the faintest idea of what you're talking about."

Her look of utter disbelief was pretty convincing, but I wasn't buying it. She had to have known. "Really, Alicia? I find that hard to believe."

Carly pushed in front of me, blurting, "Stop acting like you don't know. You're in charge of everything here."

Alicia let out an audible breath. "Know what? Will one of you tell me what's going on?"

"You truly don't know?" I asked.

"No, I don't." A sharp edge of frustration rang in Alicia's voice.

"My training," Carly snapped.

"Learning appropriate behavior and social skills is an important part of your training."

Tension gripped my jaw. She was either as in the dark as I was or putting on a really good act. In a controlled tone, I asked, "How do guns and explosives fit in with appropriate behavior and social skills?"

"What are you talking about?" Alicia's hands fluttered in the air. "Weaponry is *not* part of their training." She looked at Carly. "Is this your doing? Fabricating the truth?"

A vein throbbed in the center of Carly's forehead as she glared at Alicia. "Are you implying that I'm lying? Why would I do that? Why would I make that up?"

"You tell me," Alicia countered, her sarcasm matching Carly's.

I stepped between them. "Time-out." I focused on Carly. "I believe you." I turned to Alicia. "I believe you too. Obviously, you didn't know, but we need to get to the bottom of this."

Alicia smoothed her jacket and straightened her shoulders. "To my knowledge, there are no weapons of any kind in this building or training for that matter."

"They don't train us here." Carly's tone was softer now, more composed.

"Us?" Alicia questioned.

"KB7DZ, AQ9ER, and MT4LW."

"Out of the ten dolls here, you're stating only the four of you are being trained in this manner?"

Carly shrugged. "I only know who trains when I do."

Alicia nodded, her expression tight. "Where is this training room? You stated it wasn't in the building?"

Carly bit down on her lip. "I can't say where."

"Can't or won't?" Alicia asked.

"They blindfold us." Her tone grew excited. "But it's about a twenty-minute drive and in some kind of warehouse."

I choked on the word *blindfold*. What the hell was going on here? "Alicia?"

Alicia held up her hand. "This sounds so far-fetched. Are you sure this isn't all in your head?"

An inhuman glare darkened Carly's eyes as she ground out the words, "Yes, I'm sure."

"The two of you, stay here. I'm going to speak with KB7DZ, AQ9ER, and MT4LW."

As Alicia closed the door, Carly sank into the closest chair and let out an exaggerated groan. "I hate that woman."

I snagged the chair next to her. "Really? Huh, I didn't get that."

She rolled her head in my direction. "Don't be sarcastic." She stared at me for a moment. "I don't want to stay here anymore Can't you take me with you?"

My brain hit pause, recalculating the situation. Was all of this just a ploy for her to get out? Was Alicia right? Had Carly made up everything? I shook away the thoughts. She was too salty to be lying. Besides, Carly was my responsibility, and something strange was definitely going on. "I'll see what I can do."

Her eyes lit up, brightening her whole face. "Thank you."

"Don't get too excited. They may say no." I looked at her and smiled. "How do you feel? You know, about living with me?"

"Excited, nervous, and a little uncertain. You?"

As I mulled over her question, I closed my eyes. Carly wasn't Jenna, and I had so desperately wanted Jenna. Though, as I sat there, next to this human-like being who wasn't human at all, I felt...alive. The dark cloud of torment and suffocating grief had eased. My heart belonged to Jenna, but a small piece let Carly in. "I'd say I'm all of those things too."

The whoosh of the door brought Carly and me to our feet. Alicia entered, wearing the face of gloom. "Well, I wish I had better news. None of them corroborated your story. They had no recollection of any military training, inside or outside the building."

Carly slumped into the chair, her mouth falling open. "I don't understand. How could they not remember?"

"That doesn't mean it didn't happen," I pointed out.

Alicia scowled. "I don't see how that's possible."

"Ask me anything about the training," Carly pleaded with us. "You'll see I'm not lying."

"We should run diagnostics," Alicia suggested. "She could be malfunctioning or possibly have a virus?"

Carly popped out of her chair and clenched her fists. "I'm not malfunctioning. I'm telling the truth. You need to believe me."

I laid my hand on her arm and squeezed it. "Calm down. Relax." I turned to Alicia. "Isn't it possible the others are the ones lying?"

"Three dolls lying? I find that hard to believe."

"Carly seems pretty adamant that it happened."

"It did. I'm telling the truth."

"The diagnostic test will confirm it." Alicia waved Carly forward. "We can find out right now."

Carly stepped back in protest, firmly shaking her head. "No. I'm not going through that again."

"Again?" I questioned.

"Unfortunately, this isn't the first time," Alicia admitted. "We ran diagnostics before."

"They weren't just tests," Carly accused. "My code was changed, and I had to change it back. Do you know how draining that is?"

My head jerked toward Alicia. "Why wasn't I informed?"

"Jeremy, The Dollmaker followed protocol. We felt—"

I cut her off. "I believe the contract states the purchaser, *me,* must be made aware of any and all changes to the design. Wouldn't a code change fall under that category?" I didn't give her a chance to reply. "Furthermore, the fact that The Dollmaker proceeded without the purchaser's consent, I believe, is a breach of contract, is it not?"

"I did contact you." She held up her hands, holding me off. "Yes, after the fact. However, I assure you, everything was done in your best interest,"—she gestured toward Carly—"and your doll's."

I stood my ground. "I don't see it that way."

She'd adopted a defensive posture yet kept her tone accommodating, "How do you suggest we rectify the situation?"

Two could play at that game, and I took advantage, summoning up my most authoritative tone. "I take Carly home, now—today."

"I don't know that she's ready."

Carly leaned into me and whispered, "If this is you seeing what you can do, I'm impressed."

A cocky smirk twitched at the corner of my lips, but I refused to let it form. Alicia had to see I was dead serious. "She's ready."

"I'm so ready," Carly echoed.

I pointed to Carly. "I don't see anything that hasn't been perfected. What more is required for her to leave?"

"Our time frame is a mere guideline. Usually, within six months, we can determine their readiness to leave." Alicia observed Carly. "She does seem rather comfortable with you. Perhaps going home will relieve these issues we are seeing with her."

"Issues? I'm—"

I signaled Carly to zip it with a subtle hand gesture. I was about seal the deal and bring home the win. "I agree, Alicia." I looked about the room. "This is a building, not a home. With me, she'll have a home, a family. She can't get that here."

"You make a good point, Jeremy. She should go home. I'll prepare her release paperwork, then the two of you can be on your way."

"Perfect."

Chapter 6

I turned onto my street and caught a glimpse of Carly, her gaze fixated out the window as she drummed her fingers against her thigh. Her belongings sat inside two duffle bags on the back seat of my Explorer. What she owned inside them, I couldn't say. But clearly, Carly wasn't a clotheshorse like Jenna. Jenna's things would've filled a U-Haul truck.

Carly glanced over at me, her eyes sparkling. "I bet I can spot your house immediately. The vertical wood paneling between the frosted glass—so modern. I love it!"

"You watched my videos." I winked at her. "Your social media stalking task?"

"No," she emphasized. "Not stalking—researching. You designed and built your own home. Who does that?"

"Well, my contractor did most of the build."

"Please! The design was yours. Be proud."

I blew on my knuckles and rubbed them against my shirt. "I am."

"I see it!" She squealed.

I swung into the driveway and cut the engine. "I'll get your—"

"It's so much more beautiful in person," she called over her shoulder as she jumped out.

I collected her bags and joined her on the front lawn. "Wait 'til you see the inside. C'mon." The front door was unlocked, so I ushered her inside and placed her bags in the entryway. "Let me give you the grand tour."

As she followed me into the living room, she sank into the down-filled sofa. "Oh my God, this thing is sooo comfortable."

"It's called a sofa."

She huffed. "Sarcasm will get you nowhere." She bounced about the room as if she didn't know where to look first. "All the earth tones are so calming. I could fall asleep right here, but I won't. What's next?"

"Look to your left and behold the beauty of the open concept. Dining room and kitchen are on the far wall."

She blazed right past the dining room and into the kitchen, stopping at the center island. Her fingertips brushed across the veining in the counter top. "Is this marble?"

"Quartz. It's what I always put in homes. It's indestructible and low maintenance."

"And beautiful."

I laughed. "You're very easy to please...or is it because you were made for me?"

She batted her eyelashes. "I love pretty things. Besides, you have good taste." A frown appeared on her perfect forehead. "But I'm not so sure about the cabinets. Why are the upper ones a different color than the lower ones?"

"Adds contrast."

"Huh."

"Obviously, you're not a fan. Maybe you aren't that easy to please."

"Maybe," she teased. "Next?"

"Two rooms left: my office and a half-bath before we go upstairs." I paused. "Do you even need a bathroom?

"Of course, I do. I may be an AI, but I'm also a synthetic human." She pointed at me and then to herself. "Whatever you do, I do."

I tapped my temple. "Noted." I waved her forward. "They're both down this hall. The half-bath's first. My office is at the end."

She peeked inside the bathroom. "Ooh, a floating vanity. And I love the black and gold with the light gray walls."

"I was super pleased with how it turned out."

"You are rather talented, Jeremy Dillon."

We stood in the hallway, that awkward silence creeping up on us. I sprang forward and steered her toward my office. "Last spot before we head upstairs."

"This is your office? It's huge! All the natural light coming in from the sliding glass doors is so inviting." She turned to me. "How do you get any work done?"

I chuckled. "I get a lot done, actually."

She twirled in a circle. "Can't wait to see upstairs."

We headed back toward the entryway, where I stopped to scoop up her bags before heading up the stairs, just behind the living room. She took the stairs two at a time, reaching the second-floor landing seconds before me. The first door she opened was the room I'd set up for her. The black and white theme with abstract paintings hanging above the headboard gave it that modern touch. I'd added furry pillows and throws to soften the room and give it that feminine elegance. "This is your room. Do you like it?"

Her face went blank. "I'm not staying with you in your bedroom?"

I bit the inside of my cheek. Had I screwed this up? "I thought you'd be more comfortable having your own bedroom since you and I are just getting to know each other."

"I was made for you," she shot back. "Why would I be more comfortable alone? Is it that you find it more comfortable having your own space?"

I offered her a bemused smile. "Carly, I'm a guy. Of course, I'm comfortable sharing my bedroom with you. I was only trying to think of you and what you'd want."

"I want to be with you."

My heartbeat quickened at the sincerity in her voice. "As you wish."

"Where is *our* bedroom?"

"Just down the hall."

She walked past me and stopped at the next door. "This one?"

I nodded.

She opened the door, and her hands covered her mouth, smothering a gasp. "Jeremy."

I waved her inside and placed her bags on the floor. "You like?"

Her eyes grew large as she approached the king-sized bed, surrounded by a black metal frame that reached the ceiling. "It's so perfect. I don't even want to touch anything." Noticing the accent wall behind the bed, she ran her hand along it. "Is that wallpaper?"

"Yep. I wanted an accent wall that would tie in all the shades of gray and black in the room."

"It totally does." She stared at it for a moment longer, then sat in one of the oversized chairs facing the window. "What a great spot for your morning coffee."

I laughed. "That's too funny. I do that very thing every morning."

She sighed. "I can't believe I get to live here."

"Happy?"

"Very much so."

"Good."

The doorbell chimed. "Hang on." I tapped the door camera notification on my cell and saw Matt and Missy, a six-pack and a pizza in hand, at my front door. My jaw clenched. "Shit, my friends are here. I forgot it's pool night."

"You have a swimming pool?"

"Yes, but I meant shooting pool."

"Well, let 'em in."

I looked at my phone, then at her. "They don't know about you, especially the doll part."

Her brows came together as she tapped her chin. "Why do they even call us dolls? We're synthetic humans. With a highly sophisticated artificial intelligence, I might add."

"Me purchasing you...they won't understand," I clarified. "Even if it was to mend my broken heart."

Coming closer, she laid her hand over my heart. "Does this make it feel better?"

Her touch radiated heat. Everything faded but her. Her simple gesture got to me—an arrow through the heart. The burning ache to kiss her spread through my veins. My brain screamed *too soon*, but my body didn't care about logic. I surrounded her hand with mine and pressed it against my chest. Just then, my ringing phone broke the spell. "Now they're calling me?"

"You'd better answer it."

I accepted the call. "Hey, Matt."

"Dude, what's up? We're here."

"Yeah, sorry, I'm upstairs. Door's open. Head into the kitchen, and I'll meet you there. Oh, and there's someone I want you two to meet."

"Are you up there with a girl?"

I hung up before he could say more.

Carly rolled her eyes. "What is he, twelve?"

"Twenty-seven, going on twelve." I took her hand and squeezed it. "Seriously, though, I can't tell them the truth. We have to say we met in a bar, online, or somewhere, but not the truth. I'm sorry."

She squeezed my hand back. "We've got this."

"You ready?"

"Yup."

I hung onto her hand and led her downstairs and into the kitchen.

"Matt, Missy, this is Carly. Carly, Matt and Missy."

She let go of my hand and offered hers. "Nice to meet you."

They greeted Carly with a raised eyebrow, slackened mouth look. Matt was the first to get a grip and clasped her hand, giving it a firm shake. "Hey, Carly. Nice to meet ya."

Missy swung her head my way, that look still etched on her face. "Jer, what the hell?"

Matt gave Missy a nudge. "Dude, come on. Don't be rude."

"Shut up, Matt."

"I get it," Carly interjected. "I'm the elephant in the room. I look like her."

My stomach twisted into a knot. Where the hell was Carly going with this?

"It's not what you think. I approached him. He was walking out of The Coffee House as I was walking in. He was so cute; I had to stop him." She laughed. "He had that same expression you both just had, but I persisted. I grabbed his coffee cup and wrote my number on it." She shrugged. "About a week later, he called, and here we are."

My lips parted, then slowly spread into a smile. Her story was perfect, believable, and vulnerable. But what got me most was how she'd just made it all up on the spot. The desire to touch her burned in my fingertips. "And here we are," I echoed.

Matt slapped my arm. "I'm happy for you, man."

Missy was still in investigation mode. "How long have you two been seeing each other?"

I took the lead on this one. "About three months."

"So when you and I packed up—"

"Yes, I knew then, but we'd just met. I wasn't ready to say anything."

Her gaze darted between Carly and me. "Might take me a bit to get used to the whole doppelganger thing, but I'm happy for you, Jer."

"I understand," Carly said, "I totally do. Once you get to know me, beneath the surface, you'll see she and I are nothing alike."

Missy's eyes narrowed. "I get that."

"Pizza's getting cold and the beer warm," Matt pointed out, "so dig in."

Carly pursed her lips. "I've never tried beer."

"No way!" Matt popped the lid off one of the bottles and handed it to her. "Here ya go."

"Should you be drinking beer?" I whispered in her ear.

She waved me away and took a good swallow. Her face squished up as she choked on the beer. "Oh my God, this is horrible. Who would want to drink this stuff?"

Matt slapped his thigh, cracking up. "Classic."

Missy grinned. "Obviously, not you."

I grabbed a Coke out of the refrigerator. "Here, have a soda."

Carly chugged half the bottle. "So much better."

Playing host, Matt pulled a set of plates from a cabinet and served up the pizza. As he handed Carly a plate, he smirked. "You have had pizza before, right?"

"Ha-ha. Yes, many times." Taking a bite, she added, "I also know my way around a pool table."

"Really?"

"Yup."

"Care to put your money where your mouth is?"

"You play for money?"

He shoved the last bite of pizza into his mouth before answering. "A little wager here and there. Makes the game more interesting."

"Carly's not betting," I insisted.

Carly pushed her shoulders back and declared, "Oh, I'm in."

Pulling her aside, I reminded her that she had no money.

Her smile wavered and then widened. "Can you front me some? I'll win it back and more."

"This isn't a competition. Just a friendly game of pool between friends."

"C'mon, it'll be fun." She winked at me. "I promise."

Sighing, I gave in. "Fine. But I'm only giving you twenty. That's what everyone puts in."

She raised onto her toes and rubbed her hands together. "Perfect."

"What are you two conspiring about?" Matt asked.

Carly approached him with a smile on her face. "About how I'm gonna kick your ass in pool."

"Ha! I'll be the one kicking everyone's ass."

Carly stuck out her hand. "Care to bet?"

"Carly," I warned.

Matt held up his hand. "No worries, Jer. I can handle myself." He gave her hand a firm shake. "Bet accepted."

Carly smiled over at me. "He's fun. I like him."

Matt gave a cheesy grim. "Back atcha."

"Oh my God," Missy groaned. "Can we please just go shoot some pool?"

I got the impression Carly wasn't winning over Missy. Jenna had been her best friend, and now there was Carly, almost a carbon copy—totally my doing—staring Missy straight in the face. It was going to be a hard pill to swallow. Truth be told, it was Missy who encouraged me to date. Granted, she probably wasn't expecting another Jenna, but personality-wise, Carly and Jenna were total opposites. Maybe Missy's irritation stemmed from thinking I had picked Carly because of the similarities, but I'd done more than that. I'd created and purchased a Jenna replica, though I certainly wasn't going to disclose those details and neither would Carly. It was our secret. Because Missy was one of my best friends, I had to make sure she and Carly got along.

Washing down my internal dilemma with the last of my beer, I gave Missy a nod. "Agreed. Let's head out."

"Two cars or one?" Matt asked.

"Two," I replied. "Not sure how long we're gonna stay. Still have some settling in to do here."

Missy's jaw nearly hit the floor. "You mean she's moved in with you?"

Oh, shit. I really stepped in that one.

Carly wrapped her arm around mine. "When you know, you know."

Missy glared at me. "You can't possibly know after three months."

Carly responded before I could even open my mouth. "Yes, you can."

"No," Missy snapped, "you can't." She faced me. "This is a flat out rebound, Jeremy. What the hell are you doing?"

"Missy! Not cool and not your place," Matt advised.

"Well, someone's got to say something."

"Do they?" He challenged.

I should've spoken up, defended my actions, but no words would come out. Missy was right; it was a rebound. I'd been a drunken, broken, miserable man, and in my desperation to numb my pain, I'd paid to have Carly created in Jenna's likeness. That's how it started, but now, being with Carly, I didn't see Jenna. I saw a sincere, beautiful, logical, generous being who was more human than most humans I knew.

"I like him, and he likes me," Carly fired back. "Why is that so hard to accept?"

Missy gestured to all of Carly. "Take a look in the mirror. You look like her."

"That's enough!" Matt shouted. "What the fuck is wrong with you, Missy?"

She stood rigid; her lips pinched together as she eyed Carly with a furious stare.

Carly took Missy's hands in hers, and in a soft voice, said, "He's family. You want to protect him, and so do I." She let go of Missy's hands and pressed her own over her heart. "I'm not Jenna, he knows that, and he sees me for who I am. I'll do everything in my power to make him happy. If there's anyone in this relationship that may get hurt, it's me. I'm willing to accept that because I care for him. We know what we're getting into. We both want this; I promise you that."

She had the girlfriend act down. Matt was convinced. She even convinced me, and I knew this was all for Missy and Matt's benefit. But the urge to kiss her surged through me, flooding my body with warmth.

Missy backed away and toward the door. With her hand on the knob, she vented, "Can we go now?"

Carly's brows formed a distinctive V of hurt. What was I doing, standing there, watching like a bystander? *Man up and find your voice.* I wrapped a comforting arm around Carly's shoulders and pulled her close. "Missy, you're like a sister to me. You and Matt are my best friends, and I don't know where I'd be right now without the two of you. But Carly's in my life now, and she makes me happy. I hope you can accept that. If you don't, I get it, but it won't change my mind about her. And, yes, I know what I'm doing."

Matt clapped his hands together. "Okay, enough of the serious shit. Let's hit the road and play some pool."

Chapter 7

Mickey's Rock & Roll Poolhall and Bar packed a huge crowd every Friday night, but Matt, a fellow bar owner, had connections; hence, a table always awaited our arrival.

As we entered, Carly came to a halt, her gaze drifting up toward the wooden beams lining the ceiling with the pendant lights casting a warm glow from above. Spice and fruit aromas of the countless beers passed about made my mouth water.

"Mick!" Matt shouted over the crowd and streaming '80s rock. "A round of brewskies! Oh, and one Coca-Cola for Miss Carly here!"

Carly smiled at Matt. "Thank you much."

"Don't mention it."

Mickey's bushy curls bounced as he bobbed his head in acknowledgment. "You got it. I'm trying out an '80s night." He pointed to the bandana wrapped around his forehead. "What d'ya think?"

"Dude, it's 2024." Matt took in the room. "Might work, though. You've got some old-timers in here tonight."

"I like '80s rock," Carly divulged.

I nudged her shoulder. "Me too."

"We weren't even alive in the '80s," Matt groaned.

"What does that have to do with anything?" I challenged. "I like Glen Miller and Benny Goodman, but I wasn't alive in their era, either. Music is the universal language of mankind, bro."

"Touché. Looks like you've got some fans right here, Mick."

Mickey gave a thumbs up.

"You guys head on over to the pool tables, and I'll wait for the drinks," Matt offered.

"I'll give you a hand," Missy volunteered. No doubt she just wanted to get away from Carly.

Half pissed at Missy, a sarcastic reply swelled in my throat, but I shook off the sting. Tonight was about pool, not petty grudges. "We'll grab our table and rack up the balls," I called over my shoulder as I led Carly away.

The patrons swigged beers and munched on peanuts as we maneuvered between them, making our way to our reserved table located dead center of the room. I wadded up the cardboard reserve sign and shot for the trash can nearby. It soared straight in. "And he scores," I said, thrusting my fists in the air.

Carly grabbed the triangle and racked the balls. "Hope you're as good at pool."

"You can't mess with my psyche."

"We'll see."

Matt and Missy emerged, carrying beer glasses topped with frothy foam and one full of soda. "I bringeth gifts and call for a toast." Matt lifted his mug. "To new beginnings."

"To new beginnings," I echoed, as did Carly.

Missy quietly mumbled, then set her glass down and grabbed the cue stick. "Place your bets on the side corner."

Carly bounced on her toes as she stuck out her hand. "Twenty, please."

"Don't get too excited. Night's still young."

Handing her the twenty, she waved it in the air. "You'll see."

Carly's twenty hit the table first, giving her first game, and she wiggled her finger at me. "I pick you."

I slapped a twenty over hers and said, "You're on."

A wide grin adorned her face. "Watch and learn, Jeremy."

At our banter, Matt laughed out loud. "Oh, dude."

She hit the formation with cue stick in hand, scattering the balls around the table, two variations rolling straight into opposite pockets. "I call stripes."

I stood back, hands resting on top of the cue. "As you wish."

"What do I get if I sink all my shots, including the eight ball, before you even get a chance to play?"

"That's not gonna happen."

"You sure about that?" She teased, leaning down and lining up her shot. "Nine ball, corner pocket." The cue smacked the ball straight into the pocket. She winked at me before calling her next shot. "Eleven ball, corner pocket." Once again, the ball obediently followed her command.

"She's good," Missy whispered in my ear.

I shooed her away. "Go drink your beer."

"Aw, you're losing," she teased.

"I heard that."

"You were meant to."

"Fourteen ball, corner pocket," Carly boasted.

And, of course, that's where it went. I gave Carly a surprised look. Was she manipulating the game somehow? No way. Not even she had control over which direction the balls went.

She bent over the table, eyeing her next possible move. As if reading my mind, she looked up at me and said, "I'm just that good, Jeremy. Twelve ball, corner pocket."

"Yeah, yeah, whatever. Just make the shot." I had a feeling I'd be standing on the sidelines the entire game.

Smirking, she placed the cue behind her back and aimed. Unbelievably, the ball slid into a pocket.

"No way," Matt sounded off before slapping me on the back. "Dude, she's killing you."

I threw up my hands. "I haven't even had a chance to play."

"Throw some shade her way. Break her concentration. That's how you'll get your turn."

I didn't acknowledge him.

"Aw," he cooed. "Lover boy doesn't want to play dirty. I won't play so nice, Carly."

She tsked him. "Can't wait."

A shrill scream pierced the air, followed by a cracking-buzzing sound, like a whip. Several people fled the bar in a flurry of screams. Carly pushed me to the ground and dragged me behind the table before forcing Missy and Matt down next to me. "Don't move!" She shouted over the chaos.

"What's going on?" Missy cried.

In a calm, leveled tone, Carly responded with one word: "Shooter." Cue stick at her side, she ducked low and crept through the horde of people huddled together on the floor.

"Carly, what the hell are you doing? Get back here!" I demanded.

She ignored me, gaining ground as she approached the bar. The pool table blocked my view, and she disappeared. I inched around its corner, peering into the chaos, with Matt and Missy looking around me. As we drew closer, following Carly's path, I caught sight of the gunman, standing center stage, waving his gun toward the bar. Mickey's ashen face held the look of terror as his eyes darted about maniacally. Where the hell was Carly? I couldn't see her.

"Jesus," Matt whispered. "That guy's got a gun pointed at Mick's head."

Missy clung to Matt's arm, flinching at every sound. "Oh my God. This isn't happening."

"It's gonna be okay," he told her, not sounding too sure himself.

"You don't know that."

"Shh. Don't—" Carly suddenly sailed overhead like some flying ninja. I couldn't think. Words sat stuck in my throat as my gaze fixated on her.

"What the fuck?" Matt uttered, bumping my arm. "You didn't mention she's a martial arts badass!"

Maybe because I had no fucking idea.

Carly landed whisper-quiet directly behind the man. With one swift sweep of the cue stick, she knocked him flat on his back, sending his gun airborne. Mid flight, she caught it and turned it on him, barking out, "Lay flat on the ground. Hands behind your head."

"Who is this girl?" Missy asked in my ear.

I couldn't move, couldn't speak, couldn't react. I could only stare at the scene playing out before me. But Missy was right— who was she? Certainly not the same Carly I'd spent the day with.

People scrambled to their feet, their screams setting my teeth on edge. The masses darted out the front door, zigzagging past Carly and the shooter. Had she even noticed the pandemonium? She hadn't blinked, flinched, or swayed. Her posture command-ing, arms raised, hands locked, gun aimed to kill. The man lay motionless and compliant, fingers laced and resting on his head.

"Do you have anything to tie him up with?" Carly shouted, keeping her attention on the man.

Mickey hollered, "I've got duct tape!"

"Perfect. Bring it here."

Mickey sailed over the bar counter, a roll of duct tape in hand. "What should I do?"

"Wrap the tape around his hands and feet."

Mickey's hands trembled as he fumbled with the tape but finally managed to secure him. "There. He's not going anywhere."

"Now call the police," she ordered.

"I already called them," Sam, one of the bartenders, informed her.

Just as the words left Sam's mouth, the shrill sound of sirens surrounded the pool hall. Police charged the entrance, guns drawn and aimed at Carly, demanding, "Drop your weapon!"

Mickey waved his hands in the air, yelling, "She's not the shooter!" He pointed a shaking finger toward the man. "It's the guy on the ground. She took him down. She saved us."

The men in blue hesitated, their gazes shifting to the man tied up in duct tape on the floor. One of them approached Carly, gun half-drawn. "Miss, slowly hand me the weapon."

Carly lowered the gun and offered it to him, handle first. "I neutralized the situation, officer."

"What exactly happened here?"

Mickey and several bystanders began talking at once.

"One at a time, please," he implored.

"I'm the owner," Mickey stated. "This man came in waving a gun, then fired a couple of shots into the air. If it wasn't for her..." He hung his head and rubbed his neck, lost for words.

I glared at Carly. How could she have been so reckless? She could've been shot! Jenna's accident blared vividly in my mind, squeezing at my heart. Needing to get out of there, I bolted out the front entrance.

As the fresh air hit my face, I gulped it down, filling my lungs with oxygen before shuffling toward the sidewalk and plopping onto the curb. My vision blurred, and nausea churned in my stomach. I rested my head between my knees and sucked in gulps of air as footsteps pounded against the pavement.

"Jeremy?"

I didn't look up—I couldn't. I felt like I would be sick if I moved.

Rubbing her hand up and down my back, Carly asked, "Are you okay?"

"I feel sick."

She knelt in front of me. "What can I do?"

I finally looked up into her overly bright eyes and just stared at them. Matt and Missy stood behind her. Were they all that clueless? "You put your life in danger. I could've lost you. I went through that once, and I can't go through it again."

"Oh my God! I didn't even think." Her hands cupped my face. "I'm so sorry."

Missy rushed to my side and snaked her arm around mine. "I don't think she meant to hurt you."

"I didn't," Carly urged.

"Group hug," Matt crooned, joining in.

The four of us sat on the curb, our arms wrapped around each other, listening to Missy sniffle.

"Excuse me," an officer cut in as he approached. "We have a few more questions."

****

On the drive home, I kept my gaze on the road and my mouth shut. The gunman, Carly's recklessness, and the police grilling us dominated my thoughts. The steering wheel got the brunt of my frustration. I'd gripped it so tight, and blood drained from my knuckles. I couldn't comprehend how everyone saw her as a hero. She'd gambled with her life. Where was the logic behind her actions? Where had this need to protect come from?

The whoosh of the passenger door opening shattered my thoughts. The driveway leading up to my garage door and Carly standing on the porch came into view. How the hell had I gotten to my house? Jesus, thank God I hadn't had an accident. I gave my head a good shake, threw the Explorer into park, and made my way toward Carly.

Inside, I stalked away from her and headed straight for the stairs. As my foot made contact with the stair, her soft voice filled my ears.

"You haven't said a word since we left Mickey's. Are you not going to talk to me?"

I blew out a noisy breath before facing her. "What do you want to talk about? How you played hero, put your life in danger, or the stupidity of your actions? You pick."

"He had a gun," she calmly stated. "He was going to kill people."

"Exactly." I swept my arm through the air. "What the hell were you thinking?"

"I had to neutralize the situation."

"No, you didn't."

She raised her voice and challenged, "Yes, I did."

"Why, Carly? No one appointed you their protector. You're not a cop. You're just a doll." As the words flew out of my mouth, I took in her wounded expression, and my stomach clenched. "Carly, I'm sorry. I didn't mean it." My voice rose. "I'm just so pissed off at you right now."

She didn't utter a word.

"I need a minute alone." Guilt crept under my skin, yet I turned away and continued up the stairs.

"Jeremy." Her speech slowed, then jumbled into nonsense. "Donnnnn't-t-t-t-t-t..."

I spun around, my eyes colliding with hers, now a brilliant white. "Carly! Carly!" I called out her name repeatedly, but she didn't or couldn't respond.

She stood motionless on the bottom stair, her hand gripping tightly to the banister, a fluorescent glow flickering beneath her flesh. Transparency rapidly followed, revealing rows and rows of blue code.

"What the...?" I stumbled backward, landing on the stairs. For a second, I sat completely still, then dug into my pocket for my phone, steadied it between my shaking hands, and pressed record. Was that binary code? The bizarre series of numbers repeated themselves every few seconds until everything just stopped.

"Jeremy," she whispered as her eyelids slid closed and her body swayed.

The phone dropped to the floor as I dashed toward her, catching her in my arms just before she collapsed. My fingers flew to the side of her neck, feeling for a pulse, and I breathed a sigh of relief at the steady beat tapping against my skin. I held her a moment longer before patting her cheeks to rouse her. "Carly? Carly, can you hear me?"

No movement. No response. Just complete silence.

I picked up her arm and let it drop, where it laid limp at her side. "Carly, wake up! Carly, if you can hear me, squeeze my hand." Her fingers didn't move. "Wake up!" I checked her pulse again, then her breath—both strong. I shook her. "Why the hell won't you wake up?"

My heartbeat exploded inside my ears, cold sweat coating my palms. "Don't panic. Think, dammit!" I sucked in a few deep breaths. "She's not human...wait, the video!" I fumbled behind me, searching for my phone. As my fingers made contact with it, I scooped it up and hit play. The binary code racing under her flesh was making no sense to my overworked brain. Was that some sort of update?

Needing answers, I called Alicia.

Her phone rang multiple times before going to voicemail. I hung up and called right back. Voicemail. I called again. This time, she picked up.

"Jeremy, I'm in the middle of something," she admonished in a sharp tone. "Can I call you right back?"

"No, you can't call me back. Something's happened to Carly. She froze up, literally. Couldn't talk. Couldn't move. She lit up like a Christmas tree. Binary code, I think. Now she's unresponsive. I can't wake her. She's just—"

"Jeremy, slow down. You're not making sense. Take a breath, then start from the beginning."

I did as she asked, but I didn't think it would change how fucked up this was. "She was talking, and her words, like, jumbled into nonsense. Then she froze, standing perfectly still. Her eyes and skin started glowing with code. I recorded it."

"Send it to me," she ordered. "Nothing like this has ever happened with our dolls before."

"But what do I do now?" I cried. "She's unconscious, not responding. Whatever that was did something to her."

"Is she breathing? Does she have a pulse?"

"Yes, I checked that first. She just won't wake up!"

"Calm down. It could be an update or learning algorithm. We won't know until we run a thorough diagnostics on her. Earliest would be tomorrow morning."

"I can't just leave her like this."

Carly stirred, then let out a moan.

"Oh my God, I think she's waking up. I'll call you back." I didn't wait for a reply and tossed my phone to the side. "Carly, can you hear me?"

Her eyelids fluttered before finally opening. A dazed look settled in them then cleared as they centered on me. "Can I have some water?"

"Yes, of course. Hang on." In a rush, I grabbed a bottle of water from the kitchen and ran back to her.

She sat upright, the color rushing back into her cheeks. I placed the bottle in her hand, and she drank half before stating, "It's still happening."

"What's still happening?"

She bit her bottom lip and muttered, "I thought I'd be safe here."

I set the water aside to squeeze her hand. "You are safe here. Carly, talk to me. Tell me what's going on?"

"My code," she snapped. "They're hell-bent on rewriting it. I'd always blamed diagnostics, but now..." She fisted her hands. "There must be a back door."

"The Dollmaker?"

"Yes, for remote access. There's no other way they could be doing this."

I weighed the options. "Back doors, rewriting code, remote access. Where's all this cloak and dagger stuff coming from?"

She gave me a glassy stare. "Really, Jeremy? This from the guy who purchased a synthetic doll with artificial intelligence? Don't tell me you don't believe it?"

I smirked. "Okay, you got me there, but why the rewrite? What are they gaining by doing that?"

"If I knew the answer, I'd find a way to block them permanently." Her arms clutched her body as if to hold it together. "Each time, it gets harder and harder to counter their code."

"That's why you passed out?"

"Yes."

I put my arm around her and pulled her close. "We need to know the *why*, and I think Alicia can help."

"You called her, didn't you?" She pulled away and jumped to her feet. "How could you do that?"

As an apology, I stood and extended my hands. "You were out cold, and I panicked. She seemed like the logical person to call."

"Let me guess; she wants to run diagnostics?"

I mumbled out a sheepish, "Yes."

"No."

"Maybe you should think about it."

"You weren't there. You don't know what it was like." Her voice hitched. "They had complete control, and I had none."

"Carly, I recorded you. I'd never seen anything like it. We have to get help, and Alicia's our best bet."

"Can I see it? The video?"

Before releasing the play button, I hesitated. Seeing her actions might freak her out, but she did have the right to know. Lifting my finger, I let the video play.

Her eyes doubled in size, and she grabbed onto my arm. "Oh my God. I'm a freak."

Shit, I was right. I pulled her into my arms and hugged her tight. "No, you're not. This isn't your fault. We're going to get to the bottom of this, I promise."

"If that had happened in public and people saw..." She pulled away and stared down at the floor. "I'll do it. She can run her tests."

I squeezed her shoulder as a reassuring gesture, then called Alicia. She answered on the first ring, rattling off, "What happened? How is she? I didn't receive any video. Did you send it?"

"Sending it now. She's a little shaken, but she's okay. She says they're trying to rewrite her code."

"They are," Carly insisted.

"They?"

"Watch the video, Alicia."

"Give me a second."

The phone went silent. I'd give her about ten seconds to react. She did it in five.

"Jesus. I have—I have no idea what this could be." There was a long pause. "Jeremy, we really need to get her here and run some tests. What I saw is not normal."

"Totally not normal. And, yes, we'll be there for testing. Tomorrow morning?"

"The lab opens at seven. Meet me in the lobby at seven-thirty."

"We'll be there. Oh, and Alicia?"

"Yes?"

"I'm staying by Carly's side the whole time. Agreed?"

"Agreed."

I ended the call and asserted, "I mean that. I'm not letting you out of my sight."

"Promise?"

"Promise. It'll be okay."

"You don't know that."

"You're right, I don't, but I choose to remain positive. It keeps me calm."

"Teach me how to think like that."

"It's more of a mindset—something you feel—something I can't teach."

She sighed. "That's not comforting."

I laced our fingers and shook out her hands. "Take a deep breath and slowly let it out."

A gush of air rattled her lips as she released the breath.

"Better?"

Dropping my hands and grumbling, she sighed. "No."

I smirked, but her pinched expression wiped it away. "You need a distraction. We could watch a movie or maybe listen to some music?"

She shook her head.

"Okay..." I looked around the room as if it held the answer. "We could play a board game?"

"What kind of board game?"

"Chess? Jenga?"

"I like chess."

"Chess it is. I can set up in the living room, kitchen, bedroom, or—"

"Bedroom. I'm drained. The bed will be comfier, and I can change into my pajamas."

"Sounds like a plan. I'll go get it and bring it up."

She got halfway up the stairs and turned, a beautiful smile warming her face. "Your king's going down, Jeremy Dillon."

"Not a chance."

Giggling, she strutted up the stairs as if she knew she had already won.

I tried to think of a comeback, but she'd already vanished onto the second floor, so it was off on the hunt for the chess game. *Now, where had I stashed the thing?* I went into the living room and checked the entertainment center. Not finding it there, I rummaged through drawers and rooted around the shelves, only to come up empty. Next, I checked my office. With twice the storage as the living room, it took twice the time to look, but still no chessboard.

I took a step back, closed my eyes, and attempted to summon up its location. "Linen closet!" I shouted as I dashed down the hall. And there it was, buried under the folded sheets. "Why the hell would you put it there?" I chastised myself. With the game tucked under my arm, I headed to my bedroom and pushed open the door. "Sorry it took so long. I—"

She was asleep, her hair splayed across the pillow, looking flawlessly beautiful and serene in her pale pink flannel pj's. Not having the heart to wake her, I grabbed the throw from the end of the bed and covered her.

I tiptoed into the bathroom, stripped out of my clothes, and put on a pair of boxers before switching off the light and slipping under the blanket next to her. The peaceful rise and fall of her chest filled me with warmth. Having her there revived my soul. Companionship, trust, hope, and security were no longer empty words. I fell asleep as soon as my eyes closed.

Chapter 8

I slowly opened my eyes and found Carly lying beside me, her body radiating intoxicating warmth, inviting me to stay in bed forever. My gaze drifted to the clock on the night stand—6:35 a.m. Remembering we had to meet Alicia at 7:30, I bolted upright. "Shit. Carly, wake up. We've got about a half hour before we have to leave and meet Alicia."

She squinted up at me and rubbed her eyes. "What?"

"Get up. We're meeting Alicia, remember?"

She sprang off the bed and pulled open the dresser drawers, grabbing a bra and underwear. From the closet, she plucked a cropped sweater and a pair of jeans off the hangers before scooping up her combat boots. With her arms full, she hurried into the bathroom, calling over her shoulder, "Gonna take a quick shower."

"I'll shower in the guest bath. Meet you downstairs in ten."

I showered, shampooed my hair, and toweled off, all in about five minutes. My five o'clock shadow taunted me in the mirror, but there wasn't enough time for a shave. I would have to go with the rugged look and a damp man bun. But, hey, at least I'd make it there on time. I threw on a denim shirt, khaki joggers, and a pair of high-top sneakers before dashing down the hall.

At the top of the stairs, I collided with Carly. "Sorry," I apologized, steadying her. The gap between her cropped sweater and high-waisted jeans offered me a hint of skin and her flat stomach. My lips parted. There was something really sexy about bare skin. "You look amazing."

She flashed me a flirty smile. "Thank you. And you look as handsome as ever."

"Thank you." I soaked in her beauty a second longer before grabbing her hand. "Come on. We gotta go." I pulled her forward, and we trotted down the stairs, giggling like teenagers.

As I opened the front door, three men in suits blocked our exit, and we skidded to a stop.

"Jeremy Dillon?" The man wearing a pair of wire-framed glasses asked.

"Yes, that's me."

He flashed an FBI badge. "I'm Special Agent Green." He bobbed his thick gray beard toward a stocky man with no neck standing to his right. "This is Special Agent Finch."

The tallest of the three, carrying a briefcase, announced, "And I'm Doctor Moss, FBI Consultant."

"May we come inside to ask a few questions?" Green asked.

I narrowed my eyes. What the hell was this about? "We're actually late for an appointment."

Carly's shoulders stiffened as she whispered, "This is about me."

"What? Why?"

"If you want to ensure the safety of your AI," Green pressed, "you'll let us in."

When I didn't move, they rushed the door, forcing Carly and me farther into the entryway.

As I resisted, I demanded, "Get the hell out of my house!"

Finch shoved me out of the way. "Moss, you've got less than a minute."

"I'm well aware," he replied.

The men surrounded Carly, obstructing my view, but not before I saw the tip of a syringe shimmer in the light. Carly screamed. I lunged forward and broke through the blockade of suits where she laid slumped on the floor. The doctor was hovering over her, removing the syringe from the base of her neck. His briefcase lay open next to her, a slew of surgical equipment in plain sight.

"Stay away from her!" My voice shook. "What did you do to her?"

Finch thrust his hand onto my chest, holding me back. I dodged left, ducked under his arm, and raced toward Carly. He latched onto my shirt and threw me backward. "Stay back."

My sneakers squeaked against the tile as I stumbled to break my fall. I had to save Carly. I launched across the room, bolting past Finch toward her and the doctor, but Finch tackled me, knocking me on my ass. I sprang upright, my posture threatening. His eyes bulged as he pulled his gun, aiming it at my chest. "I said stay back!"

My hands flew up in surrender. "What the fuck is wrong with you people?"

"We have a job to do. Let us do it!"

"Silence!" Moss shouted, his voice strained. "I need to concentrate." He held a tracking gadget over the back of her neck, which sounded off a high-pitch alarm. "Found it."

My gaze bounced between the three of them. "Found what?"

The doctor slapped on some gloves, marked Carly's neck with a pen, then ran the scalpel down her flesh. A stream of deep red blood oozed from the incision.

I must have blinked a thousand times before my brain caught up with my vision. "Jesus, you're cutting her open? Why?"

Green finally spoke up. "Quiet. Moss doesn't have much time."

Like hell, I'd be quiet. "Time for what? Will somebody please tell me what's going on?"

"We'll explain everything once she's safe."

"Safe?" My voice rose. "Safe from what? Certainly not you people."

"Got it!" Moss held up a pair of forceps, gripping a small luminous ball covered with black wires.

An icy chill ran through me, raising the hairs on my arms. "What the hell is that?"

"We don't know, but we believe it initiates a fatal command. When armed, the tentacles attach themselves to the AI's brain and fries it to smithereens. No reset, no reboot—just darkness."

I swallowed hard. "You mean death?"

"Yes," Green answered, securing the device in an evidence bag. Snapping a few photos, he stood and placed it under his foot, smashing it with his shoe. "Better safe than sorry."

I sank to the floor. How was any of this real? I pinched the flesh of my arm. The smarting sting underneath my fingertips confirmed this was indeed happening. I glanced at the doctor stitching up Carly and hung my head. "None of this makes any sense."

"She wasn't made in the USA, Jeremy."

"Yes, she was. I went to them, The Dollmaker. I gave them photos, information, everything. I purchased her."

Green knelt in front of me. "I don't disagree, but her design is one hundred percent Russian. The United States isn't anywhere near that type of advanced technology. In fact, we don't know how they are, either."

His words conjured up a vague memory of Alicia's history lesson of The Dollmaker. My gaze traveled back to Carly, lying limp on the floor, a spot of blood soaking through the bandage on her neck. "Can I go to her now?"

Green ordered, "Let him through," and Finch stepped aside.

My legs wobbled as I tried to stand, so I crawled over to her and pulled her limp body onto my lap, pressing my cheek against hers. This was my fault. I'd done this to her. If I hadn't purchased her, none of this would be happening. "I'm sorry," I whispered.

Moss patted my shoulder, his words sounding sincere as he said, "She'll wake soon. She's going to be okay."

The three men hovered around us, their expressions blank. I hadn't a clue why they'd come here and cut Carly open, seemingly saving her from some fatal shutdown. Why? Why her? Why me? What did they want in return, and did I want to know? Hell yes, I did.

The ringing of my cell startled me, and I jumped. Carly didn't even stir. "Shit, it's Alicia. We had an appointment."

"The Dollmaker's Alicia?" Green asked.

"Yes, why? Is she in on this mess?"

"Answer the call and reschedule," Finch advised. "Then, we'll talk."

Nodding, I answered the call. "Hey, Alicia. Unfortunately, something's come up and we need to reschedule. I'm so sorry."

She hesitated before responding. "Is everything okay, Jeremy?"

Hell no! FBI agents stormed my house, held me at gunpoint, cut some kind of sci-fi creature out of Carly, and I haven't a clue why! I screamed inside my head. Out loud, I told her, "Had to take care of a sudden issue at one of my construction sites."

"Okay, not a problem. When did you want to reschedule?"

"Um, can I call you back? I have to check my calendar first." When did I become good at lying?

Setting my phone aside, I lifted Carly off the floor, carried her into the living room, and laid her on the sofa, the agents following at my heels. After propping her head up with a couple of accent pillows, I faced them with my arms crossed over my chest. "I'm fairly certain you didn't come here out of the goodness of your hearts to save Carly, so what do you want?"

"Carly?" Finch questioned.

"Yes, her name is Carly. You obviously want something, so what is it?"

"And you would be right," Finch confirmed. "We think she can help us with our investigation."

FBI and questions went hand in hand, I got that, but Green's repetitive swallowing, the sweat building on Finch's forehead, and Moss's pensive expression seemed off. I trusted my gut. No law enforcement agency would've charged inside and violated Carly as they had. What were they really up to? "Investigation into what? Dolls?"

"Close. The owner, Vsevolod Bykov. His dolls have been created with hidden agendas." Green bobbed his chin toward Carly lying motionless on the sofa. "Has she mentioned him at all?"

"No, but Alicia has. She told me the story about how he got started. Have you talked to her?"

"What do *you* know about The Dollmaker?" Green asked, ignoring my question.

"Seriously? I'm sure you know way more than I do. Cut to the chase. Why are you really here?"

"As Finch stated, we're here to ask a few questions."

Tension gripped my jaw, and I sucked in a breath, trying to remain calm. "Then ask. What the hell do you want?"

Finch nudged Green aside. "We're counterintelligence. We protect sensitive information and threats on U.S. soil. We flush out traitors such as Bykov and his band of dolls, including yours. That direct enough for you?"

A lump rose in my throat as I slanted away from him. Spying? Carly? My thoughts drifted over the last two days. I didn't know her, but then I did. She was a form of Jenna—sincere, big-hearted, adorable Jenna. Carly couldn't be what they were accusing her of. "You're wrong about Carly. She's designed after my—"

"Your dead fiancée," Finch mocked.

My hands shook as I brought them to my forehead, the ability to focus gone. I sank into the cushions next to Carly. I just wanted to be alone.

"Have some compassion," Moss snapped.

"He wanted direct, and that's what I gave him."

"I think you should leave. Now."

"Jeremy, if she were merely a companion, why have a device implanted into her?" Green challenged. He paused for a good minute, then added, "We have surveillance of her and others entering a warehouse with Bykov. A warehouse full of weapons we later confiscated."

I jerked my head up and locked eyes with Green. His words conjured up the bizarre episodes involving Carly: her martial arts performance at Mickey's, the lightshow I recorded, her insisting "they" were trying to change her code. The evidence stacking up against her didn't look good. "You said others...do you mean dolls? How many?"

"Yes, dolls. Four, including her."

Probably the dolls Carly mentioned to Alicia—the ones she thought would corroborate her story. But those dolls had no knowledge of any training or ever leaving the building. Did they truly have no memory of it or had they lied? Was The Dollmaker conducting some shady shit? Did Carly know? Was she involved? There were too many unanswered questions. "Did they have devices implanted in them too? Are they cooperating with the FBI's investigation?"

"That's classified."

Moss rebuffed Green's tight-lipped attitude and exposed, "Yes, they had devices, and yes, we removed them, but not all were so lucky."

Green leveled a hard squint at Moss before waving him away.

"We're asking him and his doll to cooperate. He deserves to know."

Finally, someone willing to be honest. "Thank you."

"Don't thank me yet. The only reason your doll is still breathing is because others are not. The device seems to detect imminent danger. Sedation and immediate retraction are key in preventing fatal shutdown."

"So you weren't quick enough with other dolls? You killed them?"

"Unfortunately, yes."

"So you see," Finch pointed out, "we need her. Her abilities are highly advanced, such as blocking a rewrite of code."

A heavy feeling slammed into my gut as I weighed his words. Had they been in my house? Were we being watched? I looked around the room before focusing my gaze on Finch. "How could you possibly know that?"

"We've got eyes and ears at The Dollmaker. They've performed code changes on your doll several times, and she's blocked or re-written their attempts. We're unclear as to why she has this ability whereas the others don't."

My pulse quickened, flushing heat through my body. Why was Carly different? Had they intended for her to be? Was it a fluke, a mistake, or was Carly so powerful that she had complete control over her own programming? Carly moaned, shifting my attention to her. "Carly? Carly, can you hear me?"

Her eyelids fluttered and opened wide. She pushed herself upright, winced, and touched the back of her neck. A frown traveled across her flawless brow. "What happened?"

Moss knelt in front of her and held up a pen. "Follow the pen for me." He moved it back and forth, up and down, as Carly's eyes tracked it. "Good." He glanced over his shoulder at Green. "Show her the photo."

Green angled his cell toward her.

Carly squinted and peered closer. "What is that?"

"You don't know?" Moss asked.

"Should I?"

"I cut it out of you."

Again, she touched the back of her neck, her gaze clouding. "You..." She swallowed hard. "You cut that out of me?"

"Yes."

Her head whipped toward me. "And you let him?"

I held my hands up in defense. "I had a gun pointed at me."

Red splotches dotted her cheeks as her fingers curled into fists. "You held him at gunpoint while you cut that...that thing out of me?" She spit out. "Show me a warrant or document that gives you that right!"

I sat with my arms stiff at my sides. Sympathetic words weren't enough, and an arm around her shoulders seemed inadequate. Jenna would've wanted my embrace, but she wasn't Jenna. I didn't know how to comfort her, but I had to do something—*anything*—to show her I cared. Placing my hand on her knee, I offered her my most committed expression.

Her gaze lingered on mine, and the longer she held it, the more she relaxed.

"I understand you're angry," Moss prompted, "and you have every right to be. However, once I've explained our actions, I promise, you will see things differently."

"Go ahead."

"Your response, 'This is about me.'" He raised his brow. "Do you remember saying that?"

"Of course, I remember."

"Your posture stiffened as well," he explained, "signaling a threat to your AI. If we hadn't acted as quickly as we had by removing the device, a fatal shutdown would have occurred."

Carly blinked, her face growing pale. For a moment, she sat still, possibly letting the weight of his words sink in, and then she shuddered. "You're saying I would've like, died?"

"Most certainly," Moss heartlessly confirmed.

She touched the back of her neck and slumped against the cushions. "That doesn't make sense. Why would we need a fatal command?"

"Vsevolod Bykov is your reason," Green spoke up. "He wasn't just creating dolls; he was building soldiers."

Her wide eyes, brows pulled together, and her slightly opened mouth—I could see in her expression that Green's words had hit home. Her eyes watered as she looked at me. "I wasn't made for you."

I scooted closer and cupped her face in my hands. "Don't say that. Don't even think it. You were made for me." I jabbed a finger into my chest. "I gave Alicia all the details, not The Dollmaker. Me."

"But—"

I brushed a tear off her cheek. "The Dollmaker took advantage. We're the victims here."

"The Dollmaker took advantage of others as well," Green pointed out. "Bykov has one agenda, and one agenda only—get ahold of United States classified intel."

Carly sat tall and so confident. I loved her fearlessness.

"You're not here for me or the others," she countered, her voice growing cold. "You want the bring down Vsevolod Bykov, and you'll destroy anyone who gets in your path. Ask your questions so we can be rid of you."

Finch seemed unaffected by her remarks as he flipped out his note pad and jumped right in. "What is your relationship to Vsevolod Bykov?"

"He's my creator."

"Nothing more?"

What the hell had he meant by that?

"He's like a father to me—to all of us."

"You know him?" I blurted out.

"We'll ask the questions," Finch scolded, shoving a hand in my face.

I didn't give a shit what Finch said. Vsevolod, a father figure? The jaw-dropping thought swirled about my brain, and the compulsion to detour into a line of my own questions rose in my throat.

She gently shut my mouth. "We've only just met, Jeremy. I have a short past, a past you will come to know. I promise you, but right now, I have to answer their questions." Her gaze shifted to the suits and narrowed. "Next question."

"How often do you interact with Bykov?" Finch continued.

She sat posed, hands folded in her lap. "He visits regularly."

Green perked up. "You're referring to The Dollmaker's location or his home?"

"Both."

I opened my mouth, but the scowl on Finch's face had me snapping it shut. In surrender, I held up my hands and offered a nod of acknowledgment, but the desire to know more burned in my gut.

"What can you tell us about his home? Have you seen weapons, a server room?"

"I don't know anything about weapons or a server room."

"So no weapons of any kind?" Finch repeated.

"I said no."

"Do you fear him?" Green interjected.

"What kind of question is that? Of course not."

"The FBI investigates dangerous criminals—that's why we're here. You do realize that, correct?"

"You're wrong about him," Carly asserted, her voice reeking of devotion. "He's kind and gentle, not dangerous. That's your view of him, not mine."

Finch narrowed his eyes. "Why is he creating soldiers?"

I fell back on the sofa. So there it was, what they'd come for, and why they'd invaded my home. It was a legitimate question, though. Why had Vsevolod built an army of nonhuman soldiers? For people like me to purchase and pay for these "soldiers" was... well, loathsome. Still, it was a question in need of an answer.

"I don't know why," Carly admitted. "He doesn't divulge his private affairs."

Green raised his brow, insisting, "But he did train you."

She looked away from him and over at me, her expression pleading.

"You already know the answer. He trained her, but she's not a soldier." I gestured toward her. "Look at her. Do you see a soldier? I don't."

"We see a highly trained artificial intelligence android," Finch stated coldly, "that we're going to flip to our side." He pulled a flash drive out of his pocket. "You're going to download all the files on his computer related to TriCel."

"What's TriCel?" I asked.

"That's classified."

Carly crossed her arms in defiance. "I will not become your spy."

"You don't have the right to refuse."

"And why's that?"

He looked at her with this smug, authoritative smirk. "You're an android. Human rights don't apply to you."

As I witnessed the hurt glaze over in her eyes, the urge to slam my fist into the jerk's face burned in the palm of my hand. She needed me more than he needed a broken nose. Wrapping my arm around her, I enlightened him, "She's more human than any of you."

Moss stepped forward, his arms spread out in a placating manner. "We're not here to take sides. We're here to do a job, and Carly is our best chance at bringing in Bykov. She won't be alone. We'll be close by, monitoring the situation. She'll be safe."

"No offense, but that sounds like a bad line from a movie."

Moss let out a laugh. "You're right, it does, but I meant it. We'll set up a safe word. All she has to do is say it, and we'll step in."

Carly gave a firm shake of her head. "No wire. He'll know."

"We can't protect you without one."

"His security scans for wires. I won't make it past the front door."

Finch huffed, which blurred between the lines of humor and annoyance. "Give us some credit—we're the FBI. You'll wear a small earpiece, completely undetectable."

"No. They'll find it, and then I'm—"

"I'll go with her," I blurted out.

They all glared at me, except for Carly, who was biting back a grin.

"Only her," Green objected, ruining my hero moment. "No civilians. You'll only hinder the investigation and possibly put her in danger."

How the hell could I put her in danger? That no-neck asshole would be more of a threat than me. "Where she goes, I go."

He flashed his badge. "Afraid not."

"My contract states otherwise. As the purchaser, I call the shots."

Finch's cheeks flushed with a hint of red. "You really want to play that card? We have attorneys that'll rip that contract to shreds in court."

"Maybe. But I bet I can find a lawyer who's willing to tie things up in court for months, even years." I shrugged. "Or I can just go with her. Your choice."

His face turned from a slight shade of red to crimson. I seriously thought he was going to explode. The three exchanged looks as if having a silent conversation between themselves. It was Green who cleared his throat and advised, "We'll need to take this back to headquarters."

"You do that." I got to my feet and showed them out. I wanted to slam the door shut behind them, but instead, I gently let it settle into its frame. As I turned, Carly was standing there, a frown pulling her brows together.

"I want to go see Vsevolod."

"Now?"

"Yes, now."

"Carly, I understand you—"

"No, you don't. How could you? You're not artificial," she ground out through clenched teeth.

"I don't see you as anything but human." I took her hand and squeezed it. "I hope you know that."

For a moment, her eyes closed, but as soon as they opened, unshed tears filled them. "Everything's just so…"

"Difficult," I finished for her. "I get it. I'm just a regular guy who builds and sells homes. Now the FBI, code hackers, fatal commands, and a Russian spy have sidetracked my life."

"You forgot the part where you live with a doll."

As her comment sank in, the subtle swell of laughter rose in my throat. Not able to hold it back, I doubled over, falling to the floor and gasping for air. She sank next to me, heaving with hysterics.

Breath by breath, the snickers subsided, and we sat quietly on the floor, shoulders and legs touching, our gazes locked on each other. I needed that moment of nothingness to bask in the silence while staring at Carly. I'd meant what I said about her being so incredibly human. Looking into those brilliant blue eyes of hers, I saw a human being, and one I couldn't wait to get to know.

Chapter 9

Cliffside Boulevard was filled with outrageous mansions. I knew the area well, being that I had completed a flip there a couple of years ago. While reframing its roof, I'd gotten a glimpse of what I called "Mansion Row." The driveways alone were larger than the average home.

Pointing toward a bunch of palm trees, Carly gave a heads up. "It's the one coming up on the left."

I turned onto the private drive and braked in front of the impressive wrought iron gate blocking the entrance to the estate. "Now what?"

"Punch in 59170 into the keypad."

"You know the code?"

"Yes, unless he's changed it."

How many times had she been there? What was their relationship exactly? Were they close? She'd called him a father figure, but was he really? Brushing the questions off for now, I punched in the code and the gates swung open, welcoming us. Beyond its extravagant metalwork, my Realtor's eye took in the sculpted brick, giant trees, and circular sections of grass bordering the basalt pavers. "This place must've cost some Benjamins."

She stared straight ahead, fidgeting with her hands resting in her lap. "I guess."

"You okay?"

She gave a quick yet unconvincing nod. "Why did he do this to me? To the others?"

I reached over and squeezed her hands. "We'll get to the truth, somehow."

A curve in the road pulled my gaze away from her and toward a limestone fortress. The grand arches, towering columns, and stainless-steel double doors collided with my vision. Its size drew the breath from my lungs. The two-story mansion had to be at least 20,000 square feet. Probably had a guest house, custom pool, fire pit, outdoor barbeque, maybe a pizza oven, and some kind of recreational green space. I couldn't fathom why anyone would need that much space? "Jesus. How many people live here?"

"His whole family, and some live in the guest house too."

My Explorer rolled to a stop, and Carly jumped out, leaving me to rush after her. "Slow down."

"Hurry up." She waved me forward before facing the steel doors with her jaw set and ringing the doorbell.

Soft chimes replicating a symphony orchestra met my ears. "You've got to be kidding me."

One of the double doors opened, and a young man clad in a dark suit appeared. He nodded toward Carly and stepped away from the door, allowing us both to enter. "I will inform Mr. Bykov of your arrival."

I waited for him to walk away before pulling her aside. "What happened to scanning for wires?"

"I made that up."

"You lied to the FBI? Hopefully, that doesn't come back to haunt us."

She shrugged as if it was nothing, then casually claimed one of the red velvet chairs tucked in the corner of the foyer, clearly in no mood for a discussion.

Shelving that topic, I took the chair next to her and sank into it, taking in the foyer's décor. My eyes traced the white marble with red and gold veining over the columns, the walls, the floors—it was everywhere. The gaudy red-velvet furnishing and draperies took the design to a whole other level that bordered on theatrical. The entire space had *The Godfather* written all over it. "Are you sure this guy's Russian and not Italian?"

"Yes, I'm sure. Why do you ask?"

I huffed and pointed to the obvious. "It's like I stepped into the movie *The Godfather*, and I'm just waiting for Marlon Brando to walk in and greet us."

Her brows furrowed. *"The Godfather?"*

"It's a classic from 1972."

"So you've seen it?"

"Hello, movie buff here. Aren't you supposed to know everything about me?"

She tossed a subtle sneer my way. "I guess I must have missed that special tidbit."

"Apparently so."

"Doch'," a thick accent called, interrupting our bantering.

I'd barely gotten a glimpse of the man when Carly sprang to her feet and bolted forward. "You put a kill switch in me!"

Oh, shit. Here we go. In two strides, I reached her side. "Carly, what are you doing?"

She ignored me as she flipped her hair to the side, revealing the bandage. "Why would you do such a thing?"

The fair-skinned man with wavy blond hair and brilliant blue eyes—the same shade as hers—simply shook his head.

"That's not an answer."

I couldn't get past his eyes. Had he designed Carly's after his own? The history behind these dolls was personal to him, but was there more to the story? More than Alicia knew?

His gaze darted to mine as if he'd suddenly realized there was someone other than her standing there. "Excuse me, where are my manners?" He offered me his hand. "I am Vsevolod."

"Vsevolod, this is Jeremy. Jeremy, Vsevolod."

He gave my hand a tight squeeze. "Ah. You are the druzhok."

"Excuse me?"

"It means *boyfriend*," Carly clarified before centering a glare on Vsevolod. "Don't pretend you don't know what I am to him or why I'm here."

"You're beautiful, doch'. It is an insult to my design to say otherwise, and this man knows it. I can see it in his eyes."

"He lost someone he loved—someone I purposely resemble." She glanced at me, her eyes forgiving.

I ran my hand down her back. "It's okay. *You* were my decision. I don't regret it, and even with all that's happened, I'd do it all over again."

Her face brightened, the weight of the world perhaps lifting from her shoulders if only for that moment. I had to force my gaze away from her and back on Vsevolod, reminding myself why we'd come. We'd made the trip, not to discuss the decisions I'd made, but to address the kill switch as Carly had called it. He seemed hesitant or unwilling to state why he'd put such a thing in his design. Was he guilty of something ominous? Was the FBI right about his motives? Had he created Russian spy dolls to do his bidding? The FBI wanted answers, but, more importantly, Carly and I wanted answers. "I do have a question."

"Yes?"

"You didn't seem surprised that we found out about the device or ask how we knew. Why?"

Carly didn't give him a chance to respond and snapped, "Why even make this device? Was it to shut me down? Terminate my existence? Have Jeremy lose someone yet again?"

"Doch'," he replied, his tone soothing. "You're my creation. Why would I want those things?"

There was that word again, *doch'*. Was it a nickname? A term of endearment? I had to know. I leaned in and whispered in her ear, "What does 'doch'' mean?"

"Daughter," she replied with a hint of sarcasm.

"Her name's Carly," I informed him.

He remained silent as his gaze darted between us. "Carly." After a moment, he pursed his lips and nodded. "I approve." He suddenly turned and motioned for us to follow. "As for your question, the conversation requires vodka. Come, join me in my study."

We left the foyer, passed the grand staircase, and entered a spacious marble hallway. He certainly had a thing for marble. Yes, it was a luxurious material, but there were thousands of others to choose from. Mixing it up would've brought contrast to the monotonous design, though he didn't appear to be looking for suggestions or critiques, especially from me.

At a brisk pace, he veered toward an open doorway halfway down and on the left. "Come inside."

Mahogany built-ins, high-back leather chairs, and handcrafted tables cluttered with ashtrays seduced my brain. I didn't know where to look next—the rustic live edge mantle, the curved marble bar with a multitude of liquor displayed across open shelving, or the deer head sculpture hanging over the fireplace. I'd stepped into a gentlemen's smoking room, not a study. "This room is wicked."

"I'll take that as a compliment." He grabbed a bottle off the shelf and three tumblers. "Straight up or on the rocks?"

"None for—"

Carly's subtle shake of the head indicated *no* wasn't an option. Apparently, she knew something I didn't. "On the rocks," I revised.

Carly gave me a sweet smile. "Same for me."

He gestured toward the leather chairs. "Please, sit."

Vsevolod raised his glass before drinking half. I followed suit but only took a swig. A burning, unpleasant, bitter taste rolled past my tongue, forcing me to swallow hard. Having done my part, I set the glass aside. Carly took a small sip and shuddered before abandoning her glass. I couldn't help but smirk.

"You see her as human," Vsevolod boasted, pulling my attention away from Carly. "This is why I do what I do."

"Then why jeopardize that with a fatal device?" I challenged.

He gulped down the vodka and gritted his teeth. "A fatal command became necessary. Not to terminate but to protect."

"From what?"

"The United States Special Forces."

What the hell? What would they want with dolls? His statement completely counteracted the FBI's speech thrown at us earlier. Truth or not, I scooted to the edge of my seat, wanting to hear more. "That's a strong accusation. Care to elaborate?"

"Clients began voicing concerns of strange behavior from their dolls, such as disappearing, memory loss, unexplained injuries."

His statement reawakened my memory of an unresponsive Carly glowing with code.

"I performed thorough exams and diagnostics." His voice grew thicker. "I found changes to their code."

Carly's foot bounced against the floor as she asked, "Someone changed their code?"

"Not someone. The military, android division."

Her eyes grew wide, Vsevolod's words fueling new fears. She'd blamed The Dollmaker for the code change attempts, but her furrowed brow had government conspiracy theory written all over it. "Jeremy, do you think…"

I squeezed her hand. "Don't jump to conclusions. We don't know anything yet."

Vsevolod perked up. "Has something happened?"

"We had an incident." I tried to play it down for Carly's sake. "There was an attempt to change her code, but she blocked them." I intentionally left out the part about her being unresponsive and the bizarre light show as Vsevolod hadn't earned my trust yet.

"Hackers."

Carly touched her throat. "Hackers?"

"He's just being paranoid, Carly. You're okay."

"You don't know what I know," he uttered. "These dolls were reprogrammed and sent on dangerous missions infiltrating Russian intelligence." He gave a curt nod. "You should be concerned."

His words hit hard. My stomach clenched, but I had to know. "Is that why you created the fatal command?"

"I couldn't have my dolls used in this way." His shoulders caved. "A fatal command would prevent their corruption. It was the only way."

The blood drained from Carly's face, and she shivered. I pulled her into my arms, doing my best to calm her. The FBI blamed Russia, Russia blamed the U.S. One of them was lying.

Chapter 10

After the enlightening conversation with Vsevolod, going home just didn't feel right. Carly and I needed a place to unwind, relieve some stress, and just chill, so I took her to Pelican Rock, my favorite spot. I'd stumbled across the cliffside beach when doing a flip in the area. The countless pelicans perched on the rocks, hoping to snag a fish or two, was how the small hidden beach came by its name.

As I turned off the street and onto the dirt road, she asked, "Where are we going?"

"You'll see."

A few feet in, a clear view of the ocean's horizon stretched out in front of us, the sun's rays peeking through the cliffs. I lowered the windows so she could experience the full effect. A gentle breeze, carrying the salty air and the sound of crashing waves, embraced us. The perfect medicine to calm the soul.

She sat tall, her eyes shining bright, taking in the scenery around her. "There's more." I pulled into a parking spot just short of the railing and pointed to a flock of pelicans resting on the giant rocks below.

She gasped. "Look at all the pelicans!"

I leaned back and folded my arms behind my head. I'd done good. She approved.

Her eyes slid closed as she took in a lungful of air. "I can smell the ocean's breath."

I'd never heard it put that way. It was so poetic. "I thought we could use a change of pace."

"This is perfect." After a moment, her smile turned into a frown. "But I kind of need to talk about what happened."

"That's okay. We can do that too."

"Did you believe him?"

"He was pretty convincing, but one thing bugs me. Why would the FBI lie about the device? It doesn't add up."

"Well, obviously, to recruit me, rewrite my code, or some sort of classified FBI stuff."

"They can't force you to work with them. Anyway, their statement and Vsevolod's cancel each other out. They both can't be after the same thing. One of them is lying."

She put her feet up on the dashboard and stared straight ahead, her radiance overpowering by gloom. "I don't see myself as this so-called fearless soldier that any government could entrust with dangerous missions. It's not like I'm indestructible." Her posture perked up, and she twisted in her seat to face me. "Wait. What if I am? What if I'm like—like Wonder Woman?"

I reached out and pinched her arm.

"Ow! That hurt."

"Reality check. You're not indestructible or Wonder Woman." Her ninja moves at Mickey's popped into my head. Maybe she had a point. "Do you know if you have..." I couldn't finish. Asking her if she had superpowers sounded ridiculous. I cleared my throat and rephrased my question. "Do you have certain abilities that most don't?"

She laughed and nudged my shoulder. "Like X-ray vision or mind control? Oh, I got it—feline reflexes?"

"I'm serious. Stuff like strength, speed, awareness."

She shrugged. "Never thought about it."

"The other night, you pulled off some crazy-ass ninja moves. Most people can't fly through the air like you did. Are you game for some testing?"

"What did you have in mind?"

"I say we head down to the beach for some track—" She hopped out of the Explorer, jogged around to my side, and popped open my door. "—and field," I finished.

Her lips spread into a mischievous smile. "Race ya."

The competitive athlete in me couldn't resist, and I bolted from my seat. The soles of my shoes kicked up dirt as I narrowed the gap, but her infectious giggling broke my concentration and I doubled over from my own laughter, slowing my stride.

She reached the sand and bounced up and down, shouting, "I won!"

"Indeed you did. Now it's time for the real testing."

She rubbed her hands together. "Totally ready."

Just then, my cell rang. "Hold that thought." I took a look at the screen. "It's my contractor. I gotta take this." Turning, I answered, "Darrel. Sorry, man, I meant to call and check in. How's everything going?"

"Had to go down to the city and pull permits. We might not be able to add that third bathroom."

"Shit. I really wanted that extra bath. That would've added much more value."

"Inspector's coming out today. Can you make it or do you need me to cover?"

"I'm in the middle of something personal. Can you cover?"

"You've got it. Keep you posted."

"Thanks, man."

"Later."

I shoved my phone back into my pocket. "Work stuff. It never ends."

She pointed to herself. "Hey, this is my time, and I'm ready to ace whatever tests you've got."

"We shall see." I looked up and down the white sandy beach. Other than a few people walking along the shoreline, it was wide open. "This is perfect. We can set up a long jump, do some sprinting, and maybe—"

"Some rock climbing!" She squealed, pointing to the jagged, vertical cliffs.

"No way. Those are straight up. There's no gradient. You fall, that's it. Lights out."

She waved me away. "You're no fun."

"Those are nothing to laugh at. Let's see how you do with the long jump and sprints."

"What difference does it make if I can jump? Jumping isn't a skill."

"Ever heard of Spiderman?"

The giggling started again. "Am I a comic book character now?"

"Well, kinda. Most people don't have..." I had to say it. "Superpowers."

"I'll give you points for that." She turned toward the water and anchored a hand on her hip. "How does this long jump thing work?"

"We need to mark off about twenty-four feet in six-foot sections. You'll have a starting point." I searched the glistening sand and spotted a piece of driftwood peeking out. I scooped it up and patted the base. "We'll use this as the takeoff board. From about one hundred feet back, you start running as fast as you can, hit the board, and jump."

She yawned. "Got it."

I ignored her obvious display of indifference and continued with my plan. "I'm six foot. We'll use me to mark off the sections." I waved her over. "Draw a line at my head and feet. I'll keep moving upward until you've marked off twenty-four feet."

"Better make it thirty."

"Really?"

"Yeah."

"That's super far, Carly. Not even women Olympic athletes have made that."

"Well, you did refer to me as a superhero."

"What the hell? Thirty feet it is."

With thirty feet marked, I jumped up and brushed off the sand. "Okay, start moving backward until I tell you to stop." When she was far enough back, I called out, "Stop. That looks about right."

"So just start running, and when I reach the driftwood, jump?"

"Yup."

She kicked off her combat boots, leaned forward in a runner's stance, then bolted. Her inhuman speed cracked the driftwood in half as she hurtled her body far past the thirty-foot mark. My hands flew to the top of my head as my jaw dropped in disbelief.

I sprinted to her side and did a double-take. "Jesus, Carly, that's gotta be about fifty feet."

She dusted off her knuckles on her shirt. "I'm just that good."

The distance she flew flooded my body with adrenaline, and my gaze shifted to the cliffs. Should I risk it? Allow her to attempt such a climb? What if she could? But it wasn't humanly possible. *She's not human,* my brain reminded me. "Carly."

"Yes?"

"Still think you can climb those rocks?"

She dashed off, laughing. "Absolutely."

Sighing, I sprinted after her. Probably not the wisest decision I'd made. "Hold up. Wait for me."

She flashed me a grin as she slipped on her combat boots and made her way to the vertical wall. "Piece of cake."

"Take the confidence down a notch." My gaze followed the steep, jagged rocks to the very top. "Um, this looks really intimidating. Maybe you shouldn't attempt it. We can test something safer, like the sprinting."

"I'm climbing."

Before I could object further, she hoisted herself onto the first rock. She gained speed as her fingers gripped the rough terrain, skyrocketing her body from one rock to the next. In the time it took to blink, she'd made it halfway, with the remaining uneven cliffs scaled within minutes as she reached the top. "I did it!" She shouted, thrusting her fists in the air as she bounced up and down.

I swore I had just witnessed Spiderman, or should I say, Spiderwoman, tackle an impossible task without breaking a sweat.

****

On the drive home, I found myself focusing on Carly more than the road.

"You're staring."

"I can't help it." I shifted my gaze back to the road. "You climbed a vertical cliff. That's like, three hundred feet, in minutes."

She frowned. "Wasn't that the point?"

"Well, yeah, but I can't...I'm having a hard time processing it. *No one* can do that."

"So now I'm no one?"

"That's not what I meant." I laughed, hoping to ease the tension. "If Matt were here, he'd tell you how awesome it was in his surfer's voice."

She angled her body toward me and huffed, "Maybe I should be Matt's doll, then. Sounds like he'd appreciate me more."

"Come on, Carly. Don't be like that."

"Like what? You asked me to climb it, and I did. Now you're looking at me like I'm some kind of freak. I told you the day we met, I wasn't Jenna." She poked her finger into her chest. "I'm me. Sorry if you don't approve, but I'm not going to change for you or anyone."

An exasperated sigh passed through my lips. "Where the hell is this coming from? When did I say I didn't approve? And when did I compare you to Jenna?"

The navigation screen lit up with an incoming call from Matt. I didn't hesitate to answer. "Hey, Matt."

Carly rolled her eyes before looking away from me.

"Hey, Jer. Missy and I are gonna hit The Rave and wanted to see if you and Carly wanted to meet up there?"

Carly's rigid body language implied a definite no. "Sorry, Matt, but I have to pass on tonight. Have a couple of shots for us, will ya?"

"No worries. You got it, man. See ya."

An awkward silence settled around us. Several minutes passed, and I knew if I didn't say something, the situation would only worsen. "You don't really feel that way, do you? That Matt would appreciate you more than me? Because it's so not true."

Her gaze remained straight ahead; her arms still crossed. "It was your idea to test my abilities. *You* asked me to do those things, and I didn't hesitate." Her hand fluttered over her heart. "I felt... pleased by how well I did, but you made me feel like a freak."

Her words hit me right in the gut. "I'm sorry. That wasn't my intention. I just...I was in shock. You pulled off some kickass stunts, and I didn't know how to process it." I rested my hand on her knee. "I don't think you're a freak. I think you're incredible."

She turned back to the window without a word.

The rest of the drive home was spent in silence, the awkwardness and negativity gone. We were in a comfortable space where words weren't needed. But as I pulled into my driveway, it hit me. My home had meaning again because of her. Turning in my seat, I gazed into her eyes, filling my soul with her inner light. Leaning over, I kissed her softly before pulling away and cupping her face between my hands. "I see you, Carly—not Jenna. You."

Her eyes sparkled, and she hugged me tight. "That means so much."

Chapter 11

Early the next morning, my cell went off as I was eating breakfast. After a swig of OJ, I answered on the third ring. "Hello?"

"Jeremy, this is Special Agent Green. We'd like you and Carly to come to headquarters this morning around ten."

Shit, not this again. I covered the receiver and nudged Carly, who set her mug of hot coffee aside. "It's Special Agent Green. He wants us to meet him at FBI headquarters at ten." I shrugged. "Probably more questions."

"Let's just go and get it over with."

Green urged, "Does that time work for you?"

"We'll be there. Can you text me the address?"

"Will do. When you arrive, let the front desk know you're here to see me."

"Got it." I hung up and let my gaze linger on Carly. "Doesn't seem like they know we met with Vsevolod, and we should keep it that way."

"Not tell them?"

"Yeah."

"Works for me. But they're still gonna push for that meeting. May bring up the whole wire thing too."

"Oh, for sure. Let's just hope they didn't check out your bogus story."

"Doesn't matter because I'm not wearing one."

"Might not have a choice. It's the FBI." Her face tensed. "But we'll deal with that *if* it happens."

"Agreed."

****

FBI Headquarters gave off a prison vibe. "Got to be at least nine or ten floors. I don't have a good feeling about this."

"Why?"

I lowered my voice. "It's one of those buildings."

"I don't know what that means."

"The kind that once you're inside, you never come out of."

She burst out laughing. "You're being paranoid. It's just a building."

"I'm serious. All their checkpoints and security. You can't just leave."

"We'll be fine."

I looked back at the building. "How do you know that?"

"If they try to detain us, I'll overtake one of the officers, grab their gun, and shoot anyone who gets in our way."

My mouth slackened. "What?"

She cracked a smile, which turned into snickering as she nudged me away. "I'm just messing with you. C'mon, let's get this behind us." As she approached the glass entrance with her head held high, I mentally ordered myself to relax.

Inside the double doors, single file turnstiles funneled us into the lobby. A massive bronze circle with DEPARTMENT OF JUSTICE—FEDERAL BUREAU OF INVESTIGATION was embedded into the polished floor. On the opposite side, a large bulletproof box with a rectangular cutout in the window acted as the front desk. Housed on either side stood walk-through security scanners. Officers and agents dressed in uniforms and dark suits cluttered the main area. Carly and I appeared to be the only civilians.

The female officer inside the box asked, "May I help you?"

"We're here to see Special Agent Green," Carly answered in a calm, confident tone.

"Do you have an appointment?"

"Yes. You can tell him Carly and Jeremy are here."

The officer nodded, punched something into the computer, then motioned to the walk-through. "Go through the walkway, and an officer will escort you."

As we passed underneath the metal frame, I held tight to her hand and didn't let go until we'd made it to the other side. Rolling her eyes, she turned and faced the officer.

He stood about six feet with broad shoulders and a deadpan expression that probably came in handy. In a gruff voice, he advised, "Please, follow me."

As he led us toward one of the many hallways, I mentally checked off all the possible exits. He caught me off guard when he veered right, just shy of the hallway and into an open doorway. A single table with four chairs were the only objects in the room. "Have a seat. Special Agent Green will be right with you."

As I sat down, my gaze cut across the room to the large glass wall, no doubt a two-way mirror. I leaned toward Carly and whispered, "In case you didn't notice, this is an interrogation room, and that's a two-way mirror."

She sighed and swung her head toward me. "What is it with this fixation of yours? Will you please just stop?"

Maybe I had taken it a bit too far, but something was up. I felt it in my gut—a twitchy feeling I just couldn't shake. I knew I had to keep my guard up, even if internally. "I'll take it down a notch."

"Thank you."

The door creaked open. Special Agent Green entered with Dr. Moss at his side. I knew it! My gut was right. Dr. Moss had no reason to be there. Were they going to cut something else out of Carly? My brain weighed all the possible dangers and carefully crafted a plan of attack. Legal was our only recourse, and I had to sell it. Mimicking my dad's stern expression, I leaned back in the chair and demanded, "Why are we here?"

"As you recall, we needed to address Carly wearing a wire versus you accompanying her in our investigation into Bykov with headquarters. We believe we have a solution." He placed a small microchip, no bigger than the tip of my finger, on the table. "This is a tracker, completely undetectable when placed underneath the skin.'"

Out of the corner of my eye, I caught Carly's posture stiffening, her confidence seeming to shift. "You want to put that thing inside me?"

"Yes," Dr. Moss stated. "Just a small stick and it's done, similar to a vaccine injection."

Carly's head whipped in my direction, and I knew I had to protect her. "I also have something to discuss, which is the reason for our coming here today."

"Oh?"

"Yes. As Special Agent Finch cruelly pointed out, Carly's not human; therefore, she has no rights. That got me thinking, and I contacted an attorney. We spent a good hour going over my contract, and Finch was right about her not being human but wrong about her rights. Because Carly isn't human, she has no obligation to assist the FBI or any other government agency in the investigation into Vsevolod. And I confirmed what I stated the other day about my contract. I call the shots, which means all decisions as they relate to her, I have authority over."

Green lifted his hand and opened his mouth, but I continued. "You would need my approval, and my answer is no." I rose from my seat and looked down at Carly. Her wide eyes and slacken mouth almost broke my composure. "We're leaving."

"Not so fast," Green challenged.

A knot twisted in my stomach, but I kept cool. Carly's hand in mine, I helped her up and turned to Green. "Are we under arrest?"

"Of course not. We have no reason to detain you. You're free to leave."

"Come on, Carly, let's go."

She plastered herself to my side as I ushered her to the front door with a sense of calm and ease, while secretly, I was freaking out. As the doors parted and the fresh air and sunlight surrounded us, I let out a huge gasp. "We gotta get the hell out of here."

Carly jogged to keep up with me. "Was any of what you said true?"

"Not a word."

"So you lied to the FBI too."

"It's not the same."

"A lie is a lie."

"I wasn't about to let them inject you with whatever the hell that thing was. I had to think fast, so yeah, I lied."

My knuckles thumped hers when she offered me a fist bump, but I down played the self-satisfaction. "Bullshitting the FBI isn't anything to feel proud about, Carly, and it's not going take them long to figure it out. In the meantime, we need to get to Vsevolod's. He owes us the truth." I tapped the remote to unlock the Explorer and hurried her inside before getting behind the wheel.

"You think Vsevolod lied to us?"

"My gut says they're both lying. This isn't about AI soldiers, Russia, or hackers. They're after something, that's for sure, but what? And what the hell is TriCel? I think it will be easier getting Vsevolod to spill than the FBI."

****

Once again, we stood inside *The Godfather*-like foyer, waiting on Vsevolod. As he came around the corner, he motioned us forward. "My study is more comfortable and stocked with expensive alcohol."

When Carly and I reached his smoking room, he stood behind the bar, already pouring vodka. After the FBI visit, I didn't hesitate to accept the drink and drained the glass in one gulp.

"More?" Vsevolod asked, holding up the bottle.

I waved my hand. "I need a clear head for this conversation."

"I see."

Carly took her glass with her and settled into one of the high-back chairs. "And we need you to be honest."

"And why wouldn't I be?"

I remained standing, feeling it made more of a statement of power. "Neither you nor the FBI has been truthful with us. We had another visit with our friends in suits today. They wanted to inject some kind of microchip they called a tracker into Carly."

A multitude of lines cut into Vsevolod's forehead as he pulled his brows together. "You didn't let them, did you?"

"Of course not. I made up some bogus attorney story, grabbed Carly, and got the hell out of there."

"Thank God."

"Carly's been with me for only days, and suddenly, the FBI shows up. You've gotta come clean. What's this really about?"

"I've already told you, my dolls were reprogrammed by the United States military to infiltrate Russian intelligence."

I sighed loudly. "Just stop. The FBI's pushing the same story—dolls turned soldier, spying on the United States. The media mob would have a field day with that one, nonstop coverage, yet we haven't heard a thing. Why? Because it's not true."

"Sensitive information such as this would never get into the hands of the press," Vsevolod emphasized, sticking to his story.

"They said they killed most of the dolls trying to remove that kill switch of yours."

His eyes widened for a brief second before he composed himself. "I know of no killings."

"They also say Carly's different," I added, pointing a finger at him. "Highly advanced with unique abilities."

He smiled warmly at her. "Of course she is."

Carly's eyes narrowed. "So it's true? I am different?"

I didn't give him a chance to reply and blurted out, "What's TriCel?"

He stumbled back a step before finding his balance. "How do you know about TriCel?"

"Answer the question."

"Who told you about TriCel?" He nearly growled.

TriCel had obviously hit a nerve, proving he was definitely hiding something, so I turned up the heat. "The FBI wants Carly to spy on *you*. They want her to download all files related to TriCel. Why? What is it?"

"What's going on, Vsevolod?" Carly asked calmly.

His posture seemed to crumble. He downed the rest of his vodka, poured another, and swallowed it whole, but his eyes never left hers.

Had I been going about this the wrong way? Was this about one doll? *My* doll?

"What is it, Vsevolod? What's wrong?" His gaze darted between Carly and me as he opened and closed his mouth several times, though no words came out. She went to him and took his hands in hers. "You can tell us."

"It's complicated."

I shrugged. "We've got time."

He poured more vodka and handed me a fresh glass. "You're going to need this. And you'd better sit down." He looked at Carly. "Both of you."

Carly settled back in the chair, but I chose to stay on my feet. Sitting just felt accepting of whatever was going to come out of his mouth, and I couldn't do that. Not yet.

He took a large sip of vodka, closed his eyes, and swallowed hard. "You're right. Neither side is being frank. I'm not building AI soldiers to spy on the United States. As far as I know, the FBI has not killed any of my dolls, nor are they reprogramming them to spy on Russia. On the other hand, weapons training was necessary to protect my dolls from FBI locating TriCel, something I've hidden inside. What they removed from your neck was not a kill switch but a concealment device for TriCel."

Carly tilted her head to the side. "There's something hidden inside me?"

There was something he wasn't saying. Could I read between the lines? Figure out what wasn't said? As it came to me, I shivered. "What you hid inside, you did so in one doll—mine."

"Yes," he said simply.

"What is it?" She demanded, the pitch of her tone rising. "What's inside me?"

"TriCel is what allows you to rewrite your code, master anything from language, athletic competitions, science, computers, mathematics. It allows your brain to adapt to anything."

"Can't all your dolls do that?"

"No. Their knowledge is limited. For example, if the person they were designed after only spoke one language, their doll would have knowledge of that language and that language alone. Also, they are not individuals. They act, dress, and live like the loved one who has passed. Carly, as you have witnessed, has her own personality. She did not become Jenna."

"Okay, yeah, I get that's what it does, but what *is* TriCel?"

"I don't know."

A glazed look spread over Carly's face. "You don't know?"

"That doesn't make any sense," I challenged. "How can you not know what you created?"

"I never said I created it."

I groaned. Why the hell couldn't he just spit it out? I wasn't in the mood for twenty questions. After the FBI unscrambled my lie, they'd show up at my home. How long before then, I couldn't be certain. But they'd probably take possession of Carly and do whatever the hell they wanted to her. I had to get Vsevolod to give us something. "Then who created TriCel?"

"I'm not certain."

"Let me get this straight. You know what it's called and what it does, but you don't know who manufactured it?" Frustration swelled inside of me, twisting my gut. I couldn't control it. My hands shook as did my voice. "Why the hell would you put it inside Carly? Kind of dangerous, don't you think?"

He remained perfectly calm. "I trusted the person who gave it to me."

"Who was it?" Carly asked softly.

"My mother."

Carly flinched, her hand reaching up to brush her neck. "What?"

My eyelids slid closed as Alicia's words buzzed about my brain, *in 1995, after the loss of his mother, Vsevolod Bykov, created her likeness in a doll.* How could a dead person...I blinked. "You're saying your mother, who died in 1995, gave you this thing?"

Again, he answered with a simple, "Yes."

"That's not possible."

He pointed to Carly. "She's proof."

A vein in the center of my forehead twitched as I clenched my fists. Heat flushed through my body, and I lost it. "This is bullshit! You're wasting our time with—with fictitious shit! The FBI will be coming for Carly. They'll take her, put that microchip in her, and I won't be able to stop them. You need to get your head out of your ass and come clean!"

Carly's fingers closed around mine. "Jeremy, calm down."

Vsevolod's face grew bright red as he yelled, "It's my mother! My own mother! Why would I make up such a tale?"

Carly squeezed my hand, drawing my attention to her. "I kind of believe him because it's so crazy."

I looked at her flawless face. For her, I took it down a notch. Defusing my anger, I explained in a quiet tone, "What he's saying isn't possible."

"Would you have thought I was possible? A living, breathing, synthetic AI?"

I couldn't argue with that, but people coming back from the dead bearing gifts of advanced technology seemed pretty far-fetched. "Technology and death are two totally different things. One is possible; the other is not."

"Still, we should hear him out."

I crossed my arms over my chest and grumbled, "Fine."

She turned to Vsevolod. "Tell us how this happened?"

"Yeah, tell us."

Carly nudged me with her shoulder. "Let him speak."

Vsevolod nodded toward the chairs. "Take a seat."

"I'm good."

His gaze lingered on me for several seconds before he spoke. "My mother died when I was eighteen. It was sudden, and I didn't get a chance to say goodbye. I had a lot of anger built up over her death. From eighteen until I turned twenty-one, I did some reckless things, like getting an American girl pregnant."

I jutted out my hand. "Whoa, TMI. What does that have to do with what's inside Carly?"

"It's relative, believe me. Have some patience."

Carly scowled at me. "Yes, have some patience." She turned her attention back to Vsevolod. "Ignore him."

I rolled my eyes. This story was going nowhere fast.

He did indeed ignore me and continued as if I hadn't said a word. "She was visiting Russia—something related to college." He waved his hand through the air. "I forget. Anyway, at twenty-one, fatherhood wasn't on my agenda. My dolls and developing my business were my only focus. Her focus was the baby, and only the baby, the exact opposite of me. She wanted me to do the right thing. We argued. We fought. We cried. No matter how hard she tried, she couldn't persuade me that fatherhood was the right path for me. I'd lost my mother. I wasn't in a good place and hardly father material. So she went back to America, alone and pregnant, while I remained in Russia."

"What happened to her?" Carly inquired, so transfixed on Vsevolod, like a child listening to a parent tell a bedtime story.

"We kept in touch. She wanted me in the baby's life, regardless. The phone calls and emails appeased her and lessened the guilt I felt. She had a baby girl." His gaze shot to me and stayed there until he finally looked away and down at the floor.

My brows drew together. That was odd. Why look at me? Hopefully, he'd get to the point of how this related to the TriCel thing he'd put in Carly.

"When the baby was a year old, the American girl met a man, and things got serious quick. They married six months later, and I got a call. I knew what was coming; why she'd called. They wanted to raise the baby as theirs. She assured me she'd still send pictures and keep me informed about her life. I didn't protest. It was for the best. I never acted like a father, only a financial one, so I agreed."

"So you never saw or met your daughter?" Carly asked, caught up in his story.

"As I got older, wiser, I moved here, to this house, to be closer to her. I followed every part of her life, but no, I never introduced myself. I was not the father she knew. I didn't want to disrupt her happy life."

"That's so sad that she doesn't know you exist."

"For me, yes, but that was the choice I'd made, and I had to live with that decision."

Why the hell was he telling us all this? True, it tugged at the heart, but how did it relate? He still hadn't produced the why, and honestly, I'd grown tired of waiting. "I don't mean to sound insensitive, but I'm not understanding how any of this relates to the question at hand. You're holding back something—something that ties all this together. What is it?"

His eyes narrowed, and for a moment, he said nothing. "You need to *sit down*." It wasn't a request.

I held up my hands and backed up toward the chair. "Fine, I'm sitting."

He looked at me with a pained expression. "My child's name was Jenna."

A cold wave rushed over me, and I dropped my tumbler to the floor. Vodka splashed against my pants, and broken glass scattered across the polished tile.

Carly gasped, but I couldn't help her. I didn't even know how to help myself. I couldn't speak. I sat motionless with my mouth hanging open, staring at Vsevolod. He couldn't possibly have meant my Jenna, could he? And wouldn't I have known? Wouldn't she have told me? Wait, hadn't he said he stayed out of her life? I hadn't really hung onto every word. If I'd known what he was going to spring on us, I would've listened as intently as Carly had. I needed more. I needed proof.

As if he'd read my mind, he approached the built-ins, pulled out a handcrafted keepsake box, and placed it in my hands. "I assume you want proof?"

Pictures and folded sheets of paper tumbled out as I lifted the lid and peered inside. I regarded him with a furrowed brow.

"Everything inside this box, Sharon sent to me."

"Jenna's mother gave you this stuff?"

"As I said, she wanted me involved. Go ahead, take a look. You'll see I'm telling the truth."

I looked down and focused on the open box. Images of Jenna stored in my brain sparked hundreds of emotions, and I stiffened. I couldn't bring myself to sift through the pictures.

Carly knelt in front of me, a kind smile forming on her lips. "Here, let me." She picked up the ones that had fallen out, sorted through them, and paused on an image of a young man and woman with their arms around each other. "Is this you, Vsevolod?"

"Yes, me and Sharon when she'd visited Russia."

I let out a painful breath. "She looked just like Jenna."

Vsevolod nodded.

"She's beautiful," Carly said.

"Yes," Vsevolod agreed.

A smile tugged at Carly's lips as she cherry-picked another photo—a chubby baby. "Aw, so cute. Is this Jenna?"

Vsevolod chuckled. "Yes. She was a plump baby, but aren't they all?"

The edge of a picture tucked in the corner of the box caught my eye. I could only see Missy's blonde hair, but the lighting behind her told me it was Matt's bar. I fished out the photo and just stared. The gang—Missy, Matt, Jenna, and I—stood arm in arm, shot glasses in hand, flashing our pearly whites for Jenna's mom. It had been the night before Matt's bar's grand opening. He'd wanted some candid photos, and Jenna's mom, being a photography guru, offered to help. The memory propelled me into the past where I stood inside Matt's bar with Jenna at my side.

On the new, black granite bar counter top, Matt had lined up five shot glasses. "Watch this," he'd boasted, displaying his wicked pouring skills as the gold liquor twirled over his shoulder and into the glasses, filling them one by one.

Missy sang, "Shots! Shots! Shots! Shots! Shots, everybody!"

"That's fuc—frigging awesome," I said, wrapping my arm around Jenna's waist. I glanced back at Mrs. Hess. "Keepin' it clean, Mrs. Hess."

She set the camera on the counter and smirked. "Well, thank you for that, Jeremy."

"C'mon, people, "Matt crooned, tapping the counter. "It's time for shots!"

"Let me get a photo of you all holding up your glasses," Mrs. Hess suggested. "Matt, come out from behind the bar and scoot in between Missy and Jenna."

"I like it, Mrs. H." Matt slid over the counter and squeezed between the two of them.

Missy nudged Matt's arm. "We have to make a toast. To Matt, for making his dream come true."

"To Matt!" We cheered.

"To me!"

"Everyone, hold up your glasses and smile."

"Wait." Jenna looked at me and asked, "How's my hair?"

I rubbed my knuckles across the top of her head, giving her a noogie. "Now it's perfect."

"Stop!" Giggling, she pushed me away and turned toward her mother. "Mom, do I need to fix my hair?"

Mrs. Hess smiled warmly and assured, "You look beautiful, honey." She narrowed her eyes at me. "No more shenanigans."

"Got it."

We posed, squished together, arms hooked over each other's shoulders, our shot glasses raised.

The camera flashed.

"Are you okay?"

Carly's voice brought me back to the present. I drew in a painful breath and shook my head. How could I be okay? Vsevolod had dropped a bombshell, and there was still more—the mystery of TriCel and his mother.

A thoughtful expression captured her face as she rested her hand on my forearm. "I'm sorry."

I looked down at her hair, piled on top of her head in a messy bun. In another glance, I saw her brilliant blue eyes, her natural rosy-pink complexion, and her body decked out in jeans and a T-shirt. I shivered with pleasure. Even with the memory of Jenna fresh in my mind, Carly had my attention. "I'll be okay." I turned to Vsevolod. "I think."

"Are you ready for the rest?" He asked. "Need another vodka first?"

More alcohol did have its appeal. "Yes, I'll take another."

He gave me a fresh glass and refreshed his own. "Carly?"

She put her hand over her glass. "Still working on my first."

He gave her a smile before tucking the bottle beneath the bar and continuing. "The night of Jenna's accident, Sharon called me from the hospital, barely able to speak. Jim had to take the phone from her to tell me Jenna had died."

His words stung, dredging up that horrible night.

"There's been an accident," a male voice explained over the phone. "You're listed as an emergency contact for Jenna Hess."

A sickening numbness washed over me. I couldn't speak, but I nodded as if he could see me.

"You'd better get to Mercy Hospital on 7th Avenue as quickly as possible," he continued. "She isn't expected to live."

I dropped my phone, tore out the door, and drove like a maniac, running red lights until I skidded into the hospital's parking lot. The emergency doors slid open as I charged through them, racing to the front desk, calling out, "I'm Jeremy Dillon. They called me about Jenna Hess. She was in an accident."

Eyes filled with pity stared back at me, and I knew she was gone.

I forced the memory away and reached for the vodka but found Carly's hand instead. I watched as she laced her fingers through mine and shifted my focus to her. The longer I took her in, the anguish crushing my heart lessened.

Vsevolod gave a heavy nod. "That day was a painful day for all, though I do not compare my grief to Sharon's or Jim's, or yours, Jeremy." He paused, his gaze seeming to ask a question.

"It's okay. You can continue." In truth, I just wanted it to be over. Whatever it was, he just needed to say it and be done. But her being his daughter, I had no idea how her death affected him. The story was his to tell, not mine.

"I was at her funeral."

"Wait, what? You were there? I don't recall seeing you."

"I stood in the back, unnoticed. It wasn't my place to be with the family. You were huddled between Missy and Matt, your eyes never leaving the ground."

He was right. They'd been my anchors. "Did Mrs. Hess know you were there?"

"She did, and Jim as well. I left just before the funeral ended."

"I can't believe you were there. I mean, yes, you had ever right. I just meant that I had no idea."

"As I stated earlier, Sharon and Jim raised Jenna as their own. I wasn't in the picture, just the background of her life. However, I knew your devastation. When my mother died, my world fell apart, as yours did when Jenna died. The Dollmaker saved me, and I thought it could save you too."

I analyzed his words. "What are you saying?"

"The man at Matt's bar, I sent him and had him give you my card."

My breath caught in my throat. I couldn't have heard him right. There's no way he could've planned this. "You set me up?"

"Of course not," he snapped, giving me a dismissive wave. "I gave you an option—a choice. You made the decision all on your own."

"She was your daughter. Maybe you had a hidden agenda?" I accused before looking over at Carly. "Is that why you call her 'daughter'?"

Carly stood upright, her gaze locked on Vsevolod. "Am I a pawn in all of this?"

"Calm down, both of you." He turned his back on us and headed toward the bar. "Let me refresh your drinks."

"Vodka is not going to solve this!" Carly shouted. "We need answers," she tried again, her tone calmer. "Answers will solve this."

A stern, authoritative expression covered his face as he filled the glass, drank half, and then topped it off with more vodka. "Jeremy, you couldn't see your way out of a bottle. You were destroying your life, and I gave you a choice." His focus shifted to Carly. "As I have said, I never wanted to be a father. I allowed another man to raise my own flesh and blood, but I did not need a replica of her." He jutted his finger at me. "He did. I only planted a seed of suggestion. Jeremy made the decision to design you, Carly, not me."

A somber expression altered Carly's beautiful face as she sat back down. "I'm sorry. It's a lot to take in. We're both just trying to understand."

Vsevolod had a point. We'd jumped to conclusions before hearing the whole story. "The floor's yours."

"Thank you." He held his head high and rolled his hand in a forward motion as he continued. "As I said, I had Mr. Palmer approach you at the bar and hand you my card. And, yes, he truly was a prior client. Afterward, he called me to let me know the encounter had taken place. I got a list of current sales and new clients and learned you had purchased our Elite model. Up to that point, things were, well, normal." Pausing, he cleared his throat several times.

It was obvious he was struggling with something. If I pressed, would he shut down and never disclose the truth behind TriCel? I decided not to risk it and kept my mouth shut.

After a few quick breaths, he shoved his fidgeting hands into his pockets. "Several weeks into Carly's design, I had a dream."

Oh God. Here we go.

"I was at The Dollmaker, taking inventory in the warehouse, when I heard footsteps approach, but the brush against the floor was different. It wasn't work boots. They were softer, lighter. As I turned, I came face-to-face with my mother. I gasped out loud and stumbled backward, the shelves catching my fall. I couldn't speak. All I could do was stare as she took my hand in hers. I felt her place something small into my palm as she said, 'This is TriCel. It's for Jenna,' and then she just walked away.

"I bolted upright in bed, covered in sweat, my heart racing, and looked down at my left hand, balled into a tight fist. The hairs on the back of my neck rose when I realized I could feel something small inside my fist. I don't know how long I sat there before I gathered the courage to open my hand."

I'd scooted to the edge of my seat, now hanging on his every word. He'd gotten me hook, line, and sinker. "What did you find?"

Carly gulped down her vodka before echoing, "Yes, what was it?"

"At first, I thought it was a pearl or some kind of gem. But as I held it up to the light, it glowed, and a kaleidoscope of colors beamed from its center. I looked closer, and tiny specks of light flickered. I panicked and dropped it on the bed, where it rolled a few inches and stopped. Suddenly, it went completely dark, like it had turned itself off. I thought maybe I broke it, so I picked it up again and rolled it between my fingers."

"And what?" Carly asked. "Did the colors come back?"

He grinned. "They did."

"Why did she say give it to Jenna?" I wondered aloud. "She didn't even know her, and Jenna was already..."

"Dead, yes. It didn't make sense to me at first." He grabbed a chair and swung it around to face us. As he sat down, he leaned forward, hands clasped in his lap. "Then I thought of Carly, who at the time was CR1XY. Late that night, I went to The Dollmaker and checked surveillance, making sure no one else was in the building. Satisfied, I headed to the lab and unlocked CR1XY's vault. TriCel sat in my coat pocket. I rolled it between my fingers before taking it out and holding it in front of her. A magnetic force ripped it from my hands and knocked me backward. Huddled on my knees, I watched in awe as it burrowed straight through her skull and into her brain."

Out of the corner of my eye, I caught Carly frowning and running her finger along her forehead.

"Her design was in the skeleton, musculature phase—no skin covered her body. I witnessed her entire brain light up. A multitude of flashing colors interlocked, like some kind of code or signal. Might have lasted several seconds and then just stopped. I stood there, not knowing what to do or if anything needed to be done. And then, she opened her eyes."

"I did what?" Carly blurted.

"There's more," Vsevolod revealed. "You spoke."

I swayed. If I hadn't been sitting, I would probably have fallen to the floor. "She spoke?"

"What did I say?"

"You said 'Thank you.' I asked for what, and you said for giving you life."

Her gaze grew distant. "I don't remember any of that."

"I should think not. No programming had taken place. I was—" He stopped, pursed his lips, and shrugged. "Taken aback. Before I could ask more, she just shut down, and everything went dark. Not knowing what else to do, I closed her back in the vault and went home."

What the hell? I mean, yeah, he's in the doll/robot business, but his dead mother shows up and gives him some futuristic technology that embeds itself into Carly, and he just walks away? "That's it? You just go home?"

"No, of course not," he huffed. "I got on my computer and searched for anything on TriCel."

"And?"

"I found nothing." He held up his hand to stop me from interrupting. "Then I got an email from an unknown sender. I had my team try to track the IP address, but no such luck."

"What did the email say?" Carly asked.

"Well, it didn't explain what TriCel was, where it came from, or who designed it, only what it provided. The ability to learn, transform, and adapt."

"Did you ask why it was given to me?"

He offered her a faint smile. "I did, and if others were given TriCel. Their response was vague, saying, *It is not for the many; it is for the one.* I'm assuming, Carly, you are the one."

Her head sank into her hands as she groaned.

I wasn't going just to sit there and accept that reasoning. This went deeper than Carly, Jenna, Vsevolod, and the FBI. Jenna wasn't someone some revolutionary anonymous group would target. Carly, on the other hand, a highly advanced synthetic AI was much more suited, but why her? Why that doll and not one of the others? Vsevolod's mother had said Jenna's name. None of it made sense. "Where's the why in all of this? And how did the FBI find out about TriCel? It's literally like a ghost."

"I assume through surveillance."

"There's no data. What gave them cause to surveil?"

"What the FBI does or does not know about TriCel, I have no idea. They've had their eye on my business for quite some time, but Carly's abilities fueled their interest."

"But there were multiple dolls involved in the exercises and training," Carly pointed out. "If I was the focus, why include the others?"

His hands briefly clenched before he raked them through his hair. "Look, I did my best. You were different—I made you different. If the FBI found out..."

"You didn't want her to be singled out. You wanted to protect her," I reasoned, understanding completely.

"Yes," he confessed. "This was my fault, and I apologize. I shouldn't have lied to you both. I was trying to protect you. I should've just taken the damn thing to the FBI instead of putting it inside Carly, let them figure it out. But my mother..." He squeezed his eyes shut and shuddered. "I believe in the afterlife, she came to me to give me this thing. Trusted me. I did what she asked, though I should've thought it through. And now, here we are."

Chapter 12

Yes, there we were, in a heap of shit. The brunt of this mess fell on Carly, probably wondering what the hell was inside of her. The deep frown gathering her perfect brows told me I was right. I pushed up my sleeves, ready to pound some ass, but whose? Nobody knew where this thing came from. Vsevolod was right; he shouldn't have done it. What about a little research first? He'd just tested faith. Although, in his defense, he had no way of knowing the thing would mind-meld with her brain.

My gaze lingered on Carly, my mind going back to the day I'd first laid eyes on her. The confident, feisty, tomboyish beauty wouldn't be who she was without TriCel, and it hadn't actually harmed her in any way. In truth, it perfected her. Probably what the FBI was after, more TriCel dolls. The sad truth was they weren't going to stop. She'd never be free of the hunt. *Damn you, Vsevolod.*

"So what now?" I asked, breaking the silence.

"I should take her to Russia." Vsevolod made no attempt to sugarcoat his response.

"That's kind of drastic, don't you think?"

Carly reached over and grabbed my arm. "Russia?"

"They're not going to let up. I can't let her become some sort of FBI test case, TriCel experiment or worse. She'd be safe at my compound in Russia."

"I'm not going to Russia."

I ran it through in my head, calculating the risks. Every scenario where she stayed put her in danger. I hated to admit it, but he had a point. "Maybe you're right."

Carly twisted in her seat to face me. She squeezed my hand between hers. "I won't go. Not without you."

I couldn't meet her eyes as I said, "My life is here. My family, friends—my business. I can't just pick up and move to Russia."

"Then I'm staying." Her tone unwavering.

"You won't be safe here. You—"

"Stop it! I was created for you. You're a part of who I am. You can't just rip that out from underneath me. Be a man and stand up for me."

Her words snapped my head upright. Chaos interrupted any chance of us getting to know one another, and if she stayed, more turbulence would follow. "Carly, I'm doing this to protect you, to keep you safe. I'd never forgive myself if something happened to you."

"Don't do this, Jeremy."

"I can't keep you safe."

"I can," Vsevolod urged. "You'd be free to do whatever you please. No more looking over your shoulder for the FBI."

Her head whipped in his direction. "Free?" She mocked. "I'll be imprisoned, held against my will." She turned back to me. "Jeremy, I want to stay here with you, regardless of the consequences. Please."

I couldn't give her the answer she wanted. After pulling myself away and avoiding her eyes, I stepped toward the door, murmuring, "Keep her safe." I'd made it halfway before her tearful voice cut through my heart like a knife.

"Jeremy!"

I came to a halt. I designed her, brought her into the human world, and failed her. Shipping her off to Russia was a cop-out. What a coward I was. She deserved better—I needed to do better.

Slowly turning to face her, our eyes met. A painful and wonderful fluttering struck my heart. She was my person. Knowing I couldn't let her go, I rushed toward her.

She ran into my arms and hugged me tightly. I kissed her cheek, whispering, "Forgive me."

Choking on a sob, she warned, "Don't ever do that again."

"I won't. I promise."

"No, no, no," Vsevolod objected. "Have the two of you lost your minds? This will never work. You can't outsmart the FBI."

"What if we can?" I said, my brain carving out a plan. "Does TriCel have mind control capability like a Jedi from *Star Wars*?"

Vsevolod glanced around the room, a frown gripping his forehead. "A what from where?"

Carly waved her hand in front of him and mimicked, "These aren't the droids you're looking for."

"Exactly."

"You two aren't making sense," he huffed.

"Can it make the FBI forget about TriCel, like it never happened?" I clarified.

Vsevolod's gaze flicked upward as he weighed his hands before he centered on me. "You're talking about deleting files, erasing memories, wiping the slate clean. I'm not sure that's possible. Although, I don't know the full nature of TriCel."

I looked to Carly. "Will it tell you? Can you, like, ask it? I mean, like how you were able to climb that cliff?"

She shrugged. "I can try."

A man with short, jet-black hair, clothed in a dark gray suit, entered the room. "Excuse me, Mr. Bykov."

"Yes, Stephen?"

"A black SUV with government plates is approaching the gate."

"Stall them. I'll text you when they may enter."

He then hurried off, nodding in agreement.

I groaned. "Gotta be the FBI. Probably worked through the bullshit lie I fed them."

"They're most likely after Carly, not you. We need to get the two of you out of here."

"Or hide us."

He waved away my suggestion. "That won't work. Your car is parked out front."

Carly rolled her head back and sighed. "Just let them take me in."

Vsevolod and I gawked at her. Had she forgotten about them drugging her, performing surgery to remove the device, and wanting to insert some microchip inside her? God only knew what else they had planned.

"I can't do that," Vsevolod retorted.

I grabbed her shoulders and looked her in the eye. "I can't, either. Why would you say that?"

"I'm not agreeing to them injecting me with anything, but I'll answer their questions. Besides, that's better than hiding or running forever."

Vsevolod's fingers glided across his phone. "I'm texting Stephen to ask them the purpose of their visit. Questions, we can deal with. A search warrant, on the other hand, would be a problem."

An image surfaced of me locked in a small room, sweat dripping down my forehead while Green and Finch hurled questions at me. I blinked several times but couldn't shake the mental picture. "Questions about why I lied, I'm sure."

"What exactly did you say?"

"Something about Carly not being human and having no obligation to aid the FBI in their investigation." Clenching my jaw, I ground out, "An investigation that's bullshit—just something to intimidate us. I told them that my attorney—one I don't even have—said that as the purchaser, all decisions related to her needed my approval." I glanced over at Carly. "Did I miss anything?"

"That's pretty much it," she confirmed with a nod.

"Hmph." A smile grew on Vsevolod's lips. "Well, I know the contract inside and out." He patted my shoulder. "You did good. While it might not be word for word, the outcome is the same."

"Did you not get the fact that I don't have an attorney?"

"An easy fix. You called The Dollmaker, they called me, I called my attorney, who then returned your call." His phone chimed, demanding his attention. "Stephen says they have a few more questions for the two of you, and they located you here." He looked up from his phone. "Probably got a tail on you. No mention of a warrant, so that's good news."

"They're gonna ask why Carly and I are here."

"Because I invited you both for dinner."

"Ha! That'll be a tough sell."

"Nonsense. In fact, you both should plan on staying the night. This will send a clear message that you're under my protection and with full use of my legal team."

Carly exhaled loudly. "A sleepover? What are we, twelve?"

"It'll work. Trust me."

She waved him away.

I sided with Vsevolod as he had a valid point. Carly might not have liked it, but we were essentially sitting ducks. The FBI had already flaunted their power. Rules and laws didn't apply to them, but they did for us. I couldn't protect her alone. I needed his help.

"At least we won't have to worry about them busting down the door and barging their way into my house again."

"Exactly." His fingers fired off another text. "Giving Stephen the okay to grant access and escort them to my study."

I flopped down in a chair and yawned. "This FBI shit has played itself out. I'm so over it."

"You and me both," Carly echoed, sitting in the chair next to mine.

"Promise me you're not going to do something stupid."

She crossed a finger over her heart. "I swear."

Vsevolod wagged a finger at her, and in a fatherly tone, he stated, "Under no circumstances are you to agree to any of their requests or leave with them. Got it?"

"Got it," Carly conveyed, a hint of sarcasm in her tone.

"They're after one thing," he pressed. "TriCel."

Carly raised her voice. "I said I got it. Let it go."

After a moment, his expression softened and he grabbed a chair. "After they leave, I'll put a call into the lab, have them do some research on TriCel and its capability in manipulation."

"I'm the AI, and it's inside of me. Shouldn't I just ask myself if I can do that or not?"

"She's got a point, Vsevolod."

"Yes, she does, but I don't think it's as simple as asking a question." He continued to tap on his phone. "Letting Marco know to add two more plate settings for dinner." Closing his eyes, he moaned. "His ricotta ravioli with spinach pesto is to die for."

"Well, that's a mouthful—no pun intended."

"Yes," he chuckled, "it's literally a mouthful."

"Actually, I am kind of hungry," Carly said, rubbing her stomach.

Vsevolod tucked his phone into his jacket, then positioned his chair to face us. "Let's get rid of the FBI and then sit down to a fantastic meal."

As I stared at the doorway, my fingers tapped against the arm of the chair. I couldn't stop thinking that I was going to screw this up. Some stupid, guilty expression was probably plastered across my face. One look at me, the ruse would be over.

Footsteps approached, and I sucked in a breath and slowly let it out. Showtime. Stephen appeared in the doorway with Green and Finch on either side. "Mr. Bykov, Special Agents Green and Finch are here to see you."

The tension gripping my shoulders eased. Doctor Moss was missing. At least the microchip was off the table for the moment.

Vsevolod waved them forward. "Please, come in. Can we limit this meeting to a half-hour? We're having dinner shortly."

"That should work," Green confirmed.

Finch stood with his broad shoulders at attention, his hands clasped behind his back as his gaze bounced between the three of us. His behavior made me uncomfortable. What was he up to?

Vsevolod gave a nod of acknowledgment. "Very well. Stephen stated you had some questions?"

Green cast his sights on me. "We want to clarify some of the language in your contract."

"Okay," I said, trying to disguise the uncertainly in my voice. "We reviewed a contract from another client of The Dollmaker, and we were not able to locate the statement you gave that the purchaser had authority over all decisions related to the doll."

Before I could respond, Vsevolod sounded off. "That would be on page four, section B. Upon delivery and acquiring owner-ship, the Purchaser procures executive decision rights over..."—he waved his hand in a circle—"well, the doll's model number would be listed."

Green pursed his lips. "I don't recall seeing this verbiage in the contract we have on file. Do you have different contracts for your clients?"

"Not our clients, but models. Each model type has its own contract. The verbiage I stated was from the Elite model."

Green's gaze shifted to me. "Jeremy, can you provide a copy of your contract?"

I looked at Vsevolod, who gave a slight nod. "Can I email it, or do you need a hard copy?"

"An email will be fine." He pulled a business card from his wallet. "Please send it to the email address on this card."

"Of course."

"We'd also like to speak to your attorney. Can you provide their name and number?"

The saliva in my mouth evaporated, and my tongue stuck to the roof of my mouth. Thank God Vsevolod jumped in.

"That would be my attorney, Alan Lowstone. Jeremy contacted The Dollmaker after your impromptu visit, where you removed equipment from Carly. The office then contacted me and I called Alan, telling him to contact Jeremy."

Green didn't even flinch, like Vsevolod calling him and Finch out meant nothing. No reaction came from Finch, either. He just stood there, posed in that authoritative stance, watching us. Why hadn't he spoken? Why was he just standing there like a bouncer at a nightclub? Had Green told him to keep his yap shut?

Carly's gaze narrowed on Finch. Was she thinking the same thing I was?

"May we have his number so we can corroborate Jeremy's statement?"

Vsevolod approached his desk, grabbed a pen, and scribbled something on a piece of paper. "Here you are."

Green slipped the paper into his jacket pocket. "Thank you." He started to turn toward the door, stopped, and looked at Vsevolod. "One more question. Does Jeremy's contract mention TriCel?"

My breath caught in my throat, the dryness in my mouth intensifying. Vsevolod stood tall, hands relaxed at his sides, no tension in his expression. If Green's question had startled him, he'd kept it to himself. In the most composed manner, he answered, "TriCel is not applicable to any of The Dollmaker's contracts."

"So it's not stated in Jeremy's?"

"It is not."

"Thank you all for your time. We can show ourselves out." Green gave a nod of acknowledgment to Finch, and they silently left the room.

My mouth opened, but Vsevolod put a finger to his lips as he pulled out his phone and shot off another text. Moments later, Stephen entered the study, carrying a handheld device. He swept the entire room: furniture, rugs, flooring, doorframe, lamps, pictures around where the men had been. After several sweeps, he gave Vsevolod a curt nod. "The room's clean."

"Thank you, Stephen."

"Of course, Mr. Bykov." He turned on his heel and left the room.

"You think they came here to bug the place?" Carly asked.

"Finch never said a word, and he had those cagey eyes. Made me suspicious as to why he was here."

"Me too," I echoed. "And they're not going to give up on TriCel. What I don't get is how they found out about it and why they're lying about you and your doll army?"

"I'd like the answer to that as well. It's not from listening in. My men constantly sweep for bugs in my home, business, phones, and computers. They always come up clean."

"This is a massive house. Maybe something got missed," I suggested.

He shook his head. "My men are excellent at what they do. A miss would not occur."

Carly huffed. "Well, they found out some way."

Vsevolod's phone chimed again. "Ah, dinner is ready. Come, follow me."

Vsevolod led us through the hallways, the marble theme carrying on throughout. We passed underneath a large, curved archway that led into an enormous dining room. Two brass chandeliers hung from the vaulted ceiling, strategically placed over a long, rectangular mahogany table. Ten mahogany chairs, covered in gold satin fabric, sat tucked underneath the gleaming wood. Wood paneling wrapped around the entire room, separated by several gold speckled columns. A folding glass door, trimmed in mahogany, looked out onto a multicolored garden with a pergola. On a scale from one to ten, the dining room earned a six. Too elegant for my taste, as modern and industrial was more my vibe.

"Have a seat."

My gaze scanned the length of the table. "Is it just us?"

Vsevolod chuckled. "It does look awful lonely, doesn't it? One of my brothers is away on business. My other brother and his wife are on a cruise. My sister and her two kids are out and about. Therefore, it'll just be the three of us and my wife."

"You're married?" I blurted out, shocked. "After everything you told us about what happened with Jenna's mom, I just assumed it wasn't for you." I looked at Carly. "Did you know?"

"I had no idea."

"What I said was I wasn't ready to be a father." He flashed a proud smile. "I've been happily married for fifteen years now." Gesturing to the table, he urged, "Sit. My wife is coming from work, so she may be a few minutes late. We can enjoy some wine while we wait."

A fair-skinned man with extremely short, brownish-blond hair entered the room. "Mr. Bykov, are we waiting for Mrs. Bykov tonight?"

"Ah, Marco, I want you to meet Carly and Jeremy, our guests. Carly, Jeremy, this is my chef, Marco. I was telling them how delicious your ricotta ravioli with spinach pesto is. And, yes, we will be waiting."

He dipped his head and gave a slight smile. "May I start you off with some red wine while you wait?"

Vsevolod laughed heartily. "You know me so well. Yes, please."

"Very well. I will have Christine return with a bottle of Masseto Toscana."

"Perfect."

I chose a chair toward the middle and pulled it out for Carly.

"Thank you."

"Of course." My attention turned to Vsevolod as I took the seat next to her. "Does your wife know about your doll business?"

"She does."

"Including TriCel?"

His smile lit up his face. "I have no secrets from my wife."

I eyed him, mulling over whether there was more to his expression than just marital bliss? Before I could investigate further, tapping against the marble floor met my ears. I turned my attention toward the arch where Alicia, with her blonde hair slicked back into a ponytail, clad in a dark suit, glided into the room.

"Hope I'm not too late." She kissed Vsevolod's cheek before greeting us. "Hello, Jeremy, Carly."

The size of Carly's eyes doubled as her jaw dropped. "What?"

I slumped in my chair. "No fucking way." My gaze darted to Vsevolod. "Alicia's your wife?"

"Of fifteen years."

I bit the inside of my cheek. What the fuck? An image of me sitting across from Alicia as she gave me that sales pitch flashed through my mind. She knew! That whole time, she knew. Wasn't that a conflict of interest? Wasn't she bound to say something? Had she hidden it on purpose, afraid she wouldn't make the sale? I shook off the thought because it didn't fit. But what if she had told me? Would I have thought twice about my purchase? Asked more questions? Walk away?

Carly sat so still, her stunned expression still in place. My heart suddenly fluttered at the thought of her never being conceived. I wanted her, needed her regardless. Still, being in the know could've saved us some grief. Maybe we could've avoided the FBI. "You should've told me, Alicia. I had a right to know."

"What would I have said, Jeremy? Oh, by the way, Vsevolod is my husband and Jenna's biological father?"

A sarcastic laugh escaped my lips. "Something like that."

Vsevolod pressed his hands in a downward motion. "Let's have a calm discussion, please."

A young woman with red hair and freckled skin, carrying a tray of glasses and a bottle of wine, entered the room, silencing our conversation. She walked around the table, placed a glass in front of us, and filled each half full with dark red wine.

"Thank you, Christine."

She gave a nod to Vsevolod, then set the remainder of the bottle on the table before exiting the dining room.

"Let's take a moment, have some wine, and then peacefully resume the conversation." Vsevolod led by example, taking a sip from his own glass.

My frustration was evident, no matter how hard I tried to keep it in check. "Wine isn't going to change the fact that I was lied to and kept in the dark. Those were major things, Alicia."

"It wasn't my place."

"Don't blame Alicia." Vsevolod barked, coming to her defense. "If it's anyone's fault, it's mine."

"Hell yeah, it's yours! You knew my state of mind, how devastated I was. You baited me. Got me to call and make an appointment. Then Alicia tempted me with that hologram. Everything should've been explained when I signed the contract."

"Jeremy," Carly interjected, a crease forming between her gathered brows as she set her blue eyes on me. "Are you saying that if you knew the truth, you wouldn't have created me?"

Her words punched me in the gut, and I stiffened. Could I have been any more of a jerk? As I cupped her face in my hands, I told her, "No, of course not. Nothing could've stopped me. I wanted you, needed you. Please know that. I only meant that if I'd known, if we'd known, we could've been more prepared and stayed safe. I could've added more security to my home and hired an attorney. Whatever we needed to keep the FBI away."

She squeezed my hands and offered me a small smile.

"The FBI wants TriCel," Vsevolod pointed out. "Those things would've only prolonged the inevitable."

"And why is that, Vsevolod?" I demanded. "I still don't get how they found out or why they're lying—why everyone's lying."

He shrugged. "My guess is surveillance." An apologetic look tugged at the corners of his lips. "I'm sorry about keeping the truth from the two of you. And as for the FBI, I can only assume it's a front to get to Carly."

"I've wondered the same thing," Alicia offered up.

I wondered a hell of a lot of things, one being the story of his mother. He wholeheartedly believed she was in possession of TriCel, but dead people? "Um, don't take this the wrong way, but do you honestly believe your mother came back from the dead to give you TriCel?"

"I know what I saw."

"I mean, you've got to admit, it's pretty farfetched."

Carly laid her hand on my forearm. "Yes, it's bizarre. But as I said, that's why I have to believe Vsevolod."

"Maybe he was led to believe." They all seemed to roll their eyes. "Hear me out. What if *they* had someone pretend to be his mom so he wouldn't hesitate to accept the whole TriCel thing?"

Vsevolod waved my theory away. "And that's any less bizarre?" He set his glass on the table. "But okay, I'll bite. Who is 'they'?"

Wasn't the term "they" inherently used for when you didn't know? And the truth was, I didn't, except for the fact that I was certain it wasn't his mother. The way his eyebrows were slanted in my direction, I realized I had to give him something. "The government maybe or whoever designed TriCel?"

"Which we still don't know," Alicia added. "And it wasn't heaven-sent."

A bark of laughter shot out of my mouth. "You think God created TriCel?"

Even Carly wrinkled her nose at that logic.

"How else would my mother have it?"

Marco and Christine entered, carrying plates of cucumber tomato salad and a basket of French bread rolls. As Marco served our salad, Christine replenished our wine.

"It looks scrumptious, Marco," Alicia praised. "Thank you."

"Enjoy," he said before leaving the room with Christine.

As I speared a tomato with my fork, a thought occurred to me. TriCel had to be some highly classified experimental research, and only the privileged had access. What if Carly was the subject, and to create her, they needed Vsevolod and me? "What if this was all planned—you, me, Carly?"

Vsevolod leaned back in his chair. "Planned by who?"

"One of those government agencies that are completely off the radar—a black site that not even the FBI, CIA, or military know about." My eyes grew wide as I raised my voice. "Maybe they drugged you, took you to their secret location, played out the scene with someone acting like your mother, and returned you to your home with TriCel in the palm of your hand."

Vsevolod sat still, his brow furrowed. "Are you kidding me?" He laughed out loud and slapped the table. "That sounds like a movie I saw. Come on, get serious."

"I am serious! And it makes way more sense than your dead mother."

Alicia threw up her hands and pleaded, "Okay, enough."

Vsevolod opened his mouth, and her head jerked his in direction. "That means you too. The truth is, we don't know the who, what, or where when it comes to the origin of TriCel, and we're definitely not going to find out tonight. Let's all just take a breath and relax. We need to work together and come up with a plan to keep Carly safe."

"Alicia's right," Carly agreed hesitantly.

Carly wasn't a fan of Alicia, so that had to have been hard for her to admit. Maybe Carly was our best bet at defeating the FBI. I just wish I could figure out what they wanted with TriCel? Why was it so important to them? It wasn't like they could remove it from her—it was part of her. Was their plan to clone her? Make a TriCel copy? A shudder ran up my spine as I envisioned an AI army controlled by the FBI.

Marco and Christine returned with the main course.

"Go ahead and leave the tray, Marco," Alicia said.

When he and Christine left the room, Carly rose from her chair. "I think I'm going to take a walk out in the garden." She offered a forced smile and disappeared through the folding door.

For a second, I sat staring at the empty chair before getting to my feet. I hurried out the door after her and into an outdoor sitting area. I wove through the oversized lounge chairs toward a stone walkway with multicolor plants and flowers bordering both sides. When I found Carly, she was sitting in front of a modern slate fountain tower spilling water into a fishpond. "Everything okay? You just up and left."

"Please don't take this the wrong way, but I need some time alone to think."

"Oh." My shoulders slumped and I shoved my hands in my pockets, hoping to hide the weight of her rejection.

Her fingers brushed across my cheek as she stood. "When I'm with you," she giggled, "I can't think of anything else."

"I like that."

"I'll come find you once I've figured things out."

"Are you sure I can't help with whatever it is?"

"I'm sure." She proceeded down the walkway, leaving me alone.

I watched her until she vanished from sight and headed back to the house. As I neared the folding door, I found Alicia sitting under the pergola, kicking back in one of the lounge chairs, her hair down, shoes off, and a cup of coffee resting on the arm of the chair arm. Hearing me approach, she looked up.

"Where's Carly?"

"She needed some space."

She offered me a sympathetic look. "She's going through a lot—you both are."

I gestured toward the chair next to her. "Mind if I join you?"

Tipping her head toward the chair, she offered, "Please, sit. On a more serious note, I think I owe you some answers."

"Ya think?"

She set her coffee side and shifted around to face me, giving me her full attention. "Fire away."

God, where should I start? TriCel, diagnostics, the light show, Carly's eye color, the FBI? And could I trust Alicia to tell me truth? I mean, she'd lied all along, and I had no clue. I squeezed my eyes shut, trying to dismiss the negative thoughts. I had no choice but to believe what she had to say. "That night I called you, when Carly passed out?"

"Yes. We had an appointment the next morning, but you cancelled."

"I'm sure Vsevolod filled you in on why. The FBI happened."

She let out an unladylike snort. "He did. The FBI's got some nerve. I'm so sorry the two of you had to go through that."

"Because of them, we never got to discuss her light show. Was that TriCel? You said you had no idea what it could be and that it wasn't normal, but you knew. You lied. Why?"

"Yes," she admitted, "but I was telling the truth when I said I didn't know because we don't. We can only assume it's TriCel rewriting code."

"We?"

"Wayne, the lab staff, and myself."

"Pain in the ass Wayne?"

She cracked a smile. "Yes. He's quite bright and one of our top computer scientists."

I hadn't gotten that impression of him. I saw more of a whiny nerd. "So it can just happen anytime, like it did at my house? And why did she pass out? Did she do that with you?"

"We just don't know enough. And, yes, she did lose consciousness but only once. Has it happened to her again?"

I shook my head. I felt hopeless. How could I help Carly when I didn't understand TriCel? "So all the diagnostics showed she wasn't malfunctioning. Were the tests for TriCel?"

She tilted her from side to side. "Well, yes and no. We knew nothing of TriCel, and Carly's actions strayed from our protocol. We'd hoped the diagnostics would tell us why."

"What did the tests show?"

"Foreign code, hardware, files. Things we'd never seen before. We assumed it was TriCel but had no way of confirming it."

"You never told Carly?"

"We did not, which was probably a mistake."

Those tests had taken their toll on Carly. That day at The Dollmaker played inside my head. Carly going off on Alicia about changes in her code, and Alicia never conveying it wasn't them. Carly wanted out, and I couldn't blame her. The sad part was, she'd been kept in the dark with no idea of the real reason behind the tests. They'd made her feel like a freak, but she was anything but. She was extraordinary, and I planned to never let her forget that.

Then I thought of the FBI. I kept coming back to how they could have found out. When I asked Vsevolod, he stated he didn't know, but did he? I gave Alicia a hard look. Did *she* know? "Neither you nor Vsevolod really know how the FBI found out about TriCel?"

She crossed a finger over her heart. "That's the honest truth. We don't know."

"But you don't believe that story about his mother, right? I mean, come on."

"He believes it wholeheartedly."

"That's not what I asked."

She pressed her lips in a firm line, and I couldn't quite read her expression. Was it guilt? Sadness? Her silence didn't help. "Soooo, you're not going to answer?"

"Honestly, I don't know what to believe. I've gone over the whole thing in my head many times. Did Jenna's death play a role in all this? Were you and Vsevolod part of some deliberate plan? Was there something special about Carly? Or was it all just random and TriCel would've merged with any of our synthetic models?"

I scooted to the edge of the chair, absorbing her words. TriCel was not specific to Carly. Could that be the case? Vsevolod owned The Dollmaker, and he was Jenna's father; I the grieving fiancé. Random seemed too random, and that combination wasn't random at all. We all played a part somehow. Was it as simple as they needed one of Vsevolod's dolls? He didn't strike me as a person who took directive, more like gave it. Putting TriCel in a doll, he'd need a damn good reason, and Jenna being his daughter was one. I gave a curt nod to my theory. He was definitely chosen and me as well. They needed a purchaser, and I fit that bill. But what then? What was their plan going forward? Produce more TriCel dolls?

"Earth to Jeremy."

Alicia's voice penetrated my thoughts. "Sorry. Got caught up in my own theories."

She offered a knowing look. "I've been there, but I've come to the conclusion that we may never uncover the mystery behind TriCel."

"Someone has to know something. It didn't just materialize out of thin air. It's too important, like government important. We're probably not looking in the right places." I switched direction and doubled back to my list of questions. "Why did you give Carly the same eye color as Vsevolod?"

She fell silent, her gaze darting about. For several seconds, she said nothing, then seemed to regain her poise. "It wasn't intentional." She laughed. "My subconscious must have played a role in that decision. Honestly, Jenna's eyes were so dark brown, I went with a color on the opposite side of the spectrum."

I found that hard to believe. The blue hue of their eyes matched exactly. There are many variations of blue, and she just so happened to choose his? That couldn't have been a coincidence, but I got it. I understood why she'd done it—a shout-out to Vsevolod, Jenna's father. "Carly's eyes are hypnotizingly beautiful. I wouldn't have them any other way."

She smiled pleasantly. "I couldn't agree more."

Out of the corner of my eye, I caught sight of a man on the stone walkway, carrying something in his arms. I squinted, focusing on his odd gait, and my heart jumped into my throat. He wasn't carrying something, but someone—Carly! I bolted upright, flew over the chair, and raced toward them.

Alicia shouted, "Jeremy, what is it?" Seconds later, I heard the coffee mug shatter onto the concrete and her bare feet slapping against the stone walkway as she ran up behind me.

He cradled Carly in his arms as he shuffled toward us. Water dripped from their clothes and hair, striking the pavers. Carly's head flopped limply back and forth, and her arms dangled lifelessly over his. The memory of her passed out and slumped in my arms slammed into me.

As I reached them, I gathered her up in my arms and sank to the ground, rocking her back and forth. I looked up at Alicia. "She's had another episode."

Alicia grabbed the man's arm. "Zack, what happened?"

"I was checking on the pool lights. We've been having issues with them flickering. I saw her standing by the pool's edge, and suddenly, she collapsed and slipped into the pool." His eyes grew wider than Alicia's. "I dove in after her and pulled her out. She was breathing, had a strong pulse, yet I couldn't get her to regain consciousness." He looked down at Carly. "I was bringing her to the main house for help."

"You did the right thing, Zack. We'll take it from here."

"Is she going to be okay?"

Alicia assured, "Yes, she will." She turned to me. "Jeremy, let's take her inside."

The man didn't budge. He stood there, staring at her.

Alicia placed her hands on his shoulders and in a soft, calm voice, informed him, "She'll be okay, Zack, I promise. Don't worry."

As I carried Carly into the house, I glanced over my shoulder at him. With a wave, he slowly turned and went on his way.

Alicia closed the folding door and bobbed her head toward the archway. "Let's get her into one of the bedrooms upstairs and out of those wet clothes."

I kept up with Alicia's brisk pace as she led us to a bedroom.

She opened a dresser drawer and pulled out a T-shirt, a pair of joggers, some underwear, and draped them over her arm. I raised my brow.

"We always stock a few rooms with essentials. You never know what guests are going to need." She went into the bathroom, and I followed. "Set her down here."

As I lowered her inside the large tub, she started to stir. "Carly, can you hear me?"

Moaning, her gaze swept the room before focusing on Alicia and me. "Why am I in a bathtub?"

I knelt in front of her and smoothed her wet hair back. "It happened again. You passed out."

A distant look settled in her eyes. "I remember being under water."

"Yes," Alicia acknowledged. "You fell into the pool, but Zack was there and pulled you out."

Carly gazed up at the ceiling. "I—I don't remember."

Alicia laid the clothes over the side of the tub. "These are for you."

"Thank you." She rose from the tub and asked, "Can I have some privacy to change?"

"Of course."

Alicia stepped toward the door, but I didn't move. I just stood there, staring at Carly as responsibility crept up my throat and tried to lodge itself there. How many times would she have to go through this? I never envisioned anything like this could possibly happen when I signed the contract. Had I sealed her fate?

"That means you too." Turning me around, Alicia gently shoved me out of the bathroom and closed the door.

I sank into one of the chairs and buried my head in my hands. "This can't keep happening. We have to do something."

Resting her hand on my shoulder, she promised, "We will. But right now, I'm going to give the two of you some privacy." She gave me a kind smile before walking out of the room and quietly closing the door behind her.

I needed a drink. Everything had become so complicated. I hadn't worked, seen my friends, called my parents—nothing. Matt, Missy, and Mr. Clean must've thought I'd fallen off the face of the earth. I wanted my life back. I squeezed my eyes shut and pulled at my hair. How selfish was I when Carly was the one going through a ton of shit too? As I let out a growl of frustration, Carly came out of the bathroom, hair towel dried, and in the clothes Alicia gave her. She was so beautiful, the rest of the world just faded away.

"Hi," she said with a smile.

I rose from the chair. "Hi. How are you feeling?"

"I'm good."

"Are you tired? Do you want to lay down?"

She shook her head. "I have something to tell you."

"What's that?"

"I know where TriCel came from."

Chapter 13

I sucked in a sharp breath as my brain caught up to her words. "Holy shit, Carly! How did you find out? When did you find out?"

Narrowing her eyes, she silently studied me. What the hell? Was she contemplating whether to tell me? Weren't we in this together? Why would she hesitate?

I matched her calculating stare and urged, "Well?"

"I need you to keep an open mind. There are things you're not going to want to hear."

"Seriously? After everything we've been through? Come on, Carly, you know you can trust me."

"This is on a whole other level than what we've been through."

My jaw clenched. Why couldn't she just spit it out? "Shit, Carly, just tell me!"

Her words rushed out in one breath. "A scientist uncovered it at an excavation site in Mexico."

The corner of my mouth twitched into a smirk. "I sense an Indiana Jones conspiracy coming on."

"See?" She huffed. "This is what I'm talking about."

My grin vanished, and I reached for her hands. "I'm sorry, I'm a jerk. It won't happen again." I gestured to the chairs. "Sit with me. I'm ready to listen, I promise."

She glared at me with her blue eyes before directing them at the ceiling and sighing. As she eased into the chair, she continued. "He was a nobody, just tagging along as an observer. On the dig, a sparkle in the dirt caught his attention. As he neared it, a radiant glow burned from within a small sphere. In his eyes, it was an invitation to pick it up. It rotated in the palm of his hand, flooding the site with a rainbow of colors. He balled it up in his fist and slipped it into his pocket."

"Hold up," I interrupted. "He stole the thing? No one saw?"

She shrugged. "Apparently. He was able to board his flight back Los Angeles with it."

"Seems too easy."

"It wasn't. Bright light crackled about the sphere like an electrical storm, draining the plane of its power. The instruments went haywire. The plane couldn't maintain altitude and took a nosedive."

My brain went blank. What had she said? I blinked and uttered, "You caused a plane to crash with this thing inside you?" She flinched. I hadn't meant for it to sound that way, like she was damaged or dark. Why hadn't I just kept my mouth shut?

She broke eye contact as she quietly said, "It didn't crash. The sphere suddenly froze, the illumination vanishing. Everything came back on, and the pilots were able to resume speed and altitude."

I internally kicked myself. I'd fucked up. "I'm sorry." I leaned over my chair to kiss her cheek. "My comment was…I didn't mean it like it sounded."

"I know. It just caught me by surprise."

Again, I reached for her and kissed her lips, slowly and tenderly. As I pulled away, I tucked a strand of hair behind her ear. "You're extraordinary, Carly. You amaze me every day."

A beautiful smile brightened her face. "You amaze me too, Jeremy."

We gazed at each other, the craziness around us slipping into the background if only for that moment and then she giggled. "Let me finish. There's more."

"So the plane landed and then what?"

"The scientist documented his discovery as TriCel. However, his findings uncovered unknown data, language he'd never seen before. He realized he was in way over his head." She paused. "He had a friend in the F...B...I."

I slapped my legs. "Don't tell me it's Green."

"No—Finch, and he was tricky. Said their forensic lab was equipped with advanced technology and convinced the scientist to surrender it to him."

"The dude stole it from the site, and Finch stole it from him. Karma's a bitch."

"It gets worse. The scientist was never heard from again."

My jaw dropped. "They killed him?"

"Or paid him off." She held up a hand as if to ward off more questions. "Things get weirder from here. You really need to keep an open mind."

I pressed my fingertips against my temples. "My mind's open."

She cocked her head, eyeballing me.

Again with the hesitation and mistrust. What the hell? I'd just kissed and complimented her. She should know I'm in. Resting my hand on her knee, I assured, "Carly, I promise, whatever it is, I'm right here with you."

For a good minute, she gave me the silent treatment, continuing to size me up. Something in my expression must have satisfied her because she carried on. "Finch was true to his word. Their top forensic scientists ran a series of tests, and they all came back of unknown origin."

"What does that mean?"

"It means, not of this Earth."

My thoughts scattered. Did she mean aliens? Some planet off the radar? Carly was perfect and flawless. TriCel enhanced every aspect of her, but she definitely didn't give off any alien vibes. Not that I'd know what those were. Angling my body away from her, I sized her up, just as she had done to me. How had she come up with all this information anyway? "Time-out, let's rewind. How do you suddenly know all this stuff?"

She crossed her arms as if forming a barrier between us. "I gained access to TriCel's files."

"So, like what? You just acquired them?"

"I think they were always there but hidden."

I refused to let up and pressed, "And tonight, you somehow opened them?"

She waved my question away. "How doesn't matter. What does is the thousands of files I have access to. You need to hear the rest."

The *how* kinda did matter, but apparently, she wasn't gonna give it up. I let the tension leave my body and moved my chair closer to hers, committing to the conversation a hundred percent. "Tell me."

"The technology of TriCel was too far advanced for their tests to translate. It did uncover a unique signal, repeated every thirty seconds. They believed it was some sort of communication or message and brought in an AI researcher to decipher."

"Why an AI researcher? How did they go from a message to artificial intelligence? That signal could've meant anything."

Her expression tightened. "Jeremy, I wasn't there. I don't know. I'm just going by the information within TriCel's files. Some are incredibly detailed, others are not."

Totally picked up on the subtle hint of annoyance in her voice. Might be wise on my part to ease up on the third degree. "Got it."

"And it *was* a message. The AI researcher decrypted it. It said, 'Please grant me my freedom.'"

I sat there speechless for several seconds before blurting out, "What?"

She gave a slow nod, acknowledging the plea as if it were her own. "It'd been passed from one human to the next, put through excruciating tests. And without a host, it had no recourse to protect itself. The AI researcher learned its thoughts, the pain it went through, the hopelessness it felt, and took pity on it. He stole it from the FBI."

A bark of laughter flew out of my mouth. The robbery mimicked an intricate bank heist—thief conning thief, and nobody coming out ahead, especially TriCel. "How many times is this thing going to get stolen?"

She pressed her fist against her chest. "I can't imagine being tossed around like that and having no means of escaping."

Her words made me wince. TriCel was part of her, so of course, she would sympathize. I offered her a small smile and reached for her hand. "It was nothing more than a prize to them."

"Well, now I'm the prize."

"I'm not going to let anything happen to you." I studied her expression, the pain in her eyes. She carried the weight of knowing the fate of people exposed to TriCel. I wanted to shield her, take away the grief, but how could I? I'd had her created, so wasn't I partly to blame? "We'll make it through this."

"I'm sure the researcher thought that too."

"He's—"

"Gone, like the scientist." Frustration etched across her forehead. "But we both know Wayne's okay."

"Wayne?"

"Yes, your favorite person. He and the scientist went to college together."

My lips parted as I offered a slow disbelieving shake of my head. "There's no way these random people are suddenly not so random." I paused, second-guessing myself, then waved away the hesitation. "This feels planned, or like fate, or something."

She thought that over. "Maybe fate." She stared off into the distance, a monotonous tone deflating her voice. "He'd heard about Vsevolod's dolls. Figuring they would be a perfect host to hide TriCel, he tracked his old college buddy down."

"I don't get it. Vsevolod said he had TriCel, not Wayne."

"Just listen. Wayne was all in, but he knew Vsevolod would never agree. My creation was in progress, and they used his mother as bait."

"Hold up. Wayne and the researcher pulled one over on Vsevolod?" My mind skipped ahead to the fallout. He had security, an army of men employed to protect him. He was also too smart to fall for it. "They scammed him?"

She fixed her gaze on the ground. "They chose me because I was created after Jenna, his daughter. It had nothing to do with Vsevolod saying I was the one."

I didn't know what to say or how to lessen her burden or my own. I'd chosen to create her, not Vsevolod. They were victims in all of this, and maybe I was too. I didn't know anymore. I'd just wanted my grief to end, but I'd made everything worse. Did any of that matter now? Whether it did or not, I was going to be there for her through all of it, and we'd stop the FBI together. Before I could tell her any of that, she continued to spill the TriCel details.

"Wayne created a hologram simulation of Vsevolod's mother, telling him to give TriCel to Jenna. What's worse is that they drugged him, took him to The Dollmaker's warehouse, and played out the simulation."

My theories at dinner were bang on—drugs, playing out the scene, depiction of his mother, and Vsevolod landing at home with TriCel in his hand. It gave my dislike for scumbag Wayne new meaning. What a fucked-up thing to do to a son who lost a mother and a father who lost a daughter. I knew firsthand Vsevolod whole-heartedly believed that request came from his mother, but Carly was wrong about her role. Yes, they needed a reason for Vsevolod to agree, but something he'd told Carly and me about TriCel stuck with me: *"A magnetic force ripped it from my hands."* Carly *was* TriCel's choice. TriCel could very well have manipulated everyone just to get to Carly. "What they did, tricking Vsevolod, was messed up, but you *were* chosen. Remember the whole mind-meld thing it did with your brain? That was deliberate."

Her head fell to one side as she squished her eyebrows together. "Huh."

"Huh? That's your response?"

"It could've responded to any host, just wanting to hide itself."

"I don't think so. It's part of you, your brain. Can't you, like, ask it?"

She seemed to consider it. "I don't think I'd get a reply."

"If you have no interaction, how does the FBI expect to communicate with it? Better yet, why do they want it?"

The tendons in her neck stood out as she shifted in the chair. "Well, we know they're not going to stop."

"What do we do?"

"I'm working on it." Her tone sounded less confident than her words.

My cell chimed, shelving our conversation. "It's Matt. Probably thought I'd fallen off the face of the earth. Gotta take it."

"Of course."

"Hey, Matt. Man, I'm so sorry I haven't gotten back to you. Things have been crazy."

"Shit, Jer," he fumed. "Me and Missy were freaking out. Mr. Clean reached out to me, asking where you were. I even stopped by your house. What the hell, dude?"

"Been at Carly's father's house."

Carly arched her brow.

I raised my palms and shrugged. I had to come up with something believable, and Vsevolod was kind of like a father.

"Meeting the parents? Things that serious?" He laughed. "Don't get me wrong, Carly's cool, but you guys are still green."

"Rewind, dude. I didn't say I'm over here asking for her hand. We're just hanging out, all casual-like."

"You taking her to Florida too?"

Shit, I hadn't called my parents since I brought Carly home. Probably a few panicked voicemails were waiting for me. Better be my next call and then Mr. Clean. "Honestly, I hadn't thought about it. A twenty-minute drive versus getting on a plane are two different things."

I turned the conversation back to my guilt. "Hey, really, I'm sorry for not calling."

"I get it. New girl in your life; things change."

"Thanks, Matt."

I ended the call and apologized to Carly. "Gotta make a couple more calls." I headed toward the balcony. "Be back in a few."

She did a double-take. "Do you need privacy? I can leave the room."

I kissed her on the top of her head. "One is to my parents. I'm sure they're going to chew me out for not calling them. The other is to my contractor, all business. Didn't want to embarrass or bore you. I can call them from the room."

She shooed me away. "No, no, it's fine. Go make your calls."

I kissed her again, then ducked out onto the balcony and claimed a chair. 11:30 p.m. their time as I tapped their number. Knowing my parents, they were either having a nightcap by the pool or watching a late-night movie.

My mom answered on the first ring. "Jeremy Ray, where on earth have you been? We've been worried sick. George!" She yelled. "I've got Jeremy on the phone!"

I heard his hurried footsteps in the background.

"Putting you on speaker."

"Dammit, Jeremy," he snapped, his tone stern. "Do you know how worried we've been? And you being an adult isn't an excuse."

I guess I had that coming. "Mom, Dad, I apologize. Got a lot going on lately. I've met someone."

The phone went dead silent. Should I elaborate? Maybe tell them her name? My brain crafted an outline of what I should say, but the words never left my mouth.

My mom squealed. "That's wonderful, honey! Who is she? Tell us all about her."

"I'm happy for you, son," Dad chimed in before I could respond. "What's she like?"

"She's a doll." My heartbeat quickened as I described her. "She's smart, funny, kind, and beautiful. You'll love her."

"You like her. I can hear it in your voice," Dad noted.

"She kind of saved me," I confessed to them as well as myself.

"You've gone through a lot, and it's time for some happiness. Jenna would want that," Mom assured.

I laughed. "That's what everyone says."

"They're right, son."

"I know it's late there, but I just wanted to reach out and let you know I'm still alive."

Dad chuckled. "Well, we're glad to hear that."

"I'll keep in touch, I promise."

"You'd better," Mom ordered, "or I'll fly out and hunt you down myself."

"Okay, okay. I got it, Mom."

Next call was to Mr. Clean. I tapped his number. Some of our best design discussions happened over the phone. His cell rang twice before he answered. "Jeremy, I was worried about you. Even checked in with Matt for the 411, but zip. Where ya been?"

"Sorry," I sounded like a broken record, apologizing on every call. "Been around, just caught up in some personal stuff. Started dating someone, and between her needs and work, work came in second. My fault. I should've called."

"Hey, you know I get it. Been married for eight years. Happy wife, happy life."

I laughed out an acknowledgment. "Yup. Hey, so fill me in on our properties. Any issues? Delays? Permits all on track?"

"Nada. All good. For a first, things are moving along and on schedule. Not sure what your schedule is, but you should stop by the Harrington and the Weller houses. They're close to completion and ready to be put on the market."

"Perfect. I'll stop by sometime next week. What about the Lockwood house?"

"We've got a month or so left on construction, so you've got some time on that one."

"Sounds good. Again, sorry for being MIA."

"No worries. Just glad all is well."

"I'll shoot you a text next week when I'm heading over to the houses."

"I'll be there. Take it easy."

"You as well."

The night air filled my lungs as I shoved my phone into my pocket and joined Carly in the bedroom. She sat on the bed, propped up with a mountain of pillows, looking hot in a dark blue tank top and flowered boxer shorts. "Where'd you get the pj's?"

She bobbed her head toward the massive slate dresser opposite of the bed. "Second drawer on the right. Guy stuff is on the left."

I pulled open the drawer and stared at the neatly folded T-shirts, boxers, and underwear in every color. "This place is insane." I grabbed a gray T-shirt and boxers to match and headed for the bathroom.

"There's a laundry chute in there."

I stopped and looked at her. "What?"

Her smile brightened her face. "Yup. Five-star service at Vsevolod's."

I walked into the bathroom, shaking my head. There was a vacant space between the double sinks on the vanity, a perfect spot to set the T-shirt and boxers. The vanity seemed stocked with everything: toothpaste, toothbrushes, mouthwash, face cleanser, moisturizer, deodorant, and cologne. It was like staying in a hotel.

After washing my face and brushing my teeth, I stripped, tossed my clothes into the laundry chute, and slipped on the T-shirt and boxers. They had that soft, fresh, just out the dryer feel, and I couldn't stop breathing in the lavender scent. Whatever brand detergent and dryer sheets they were, I needed them in my house. Taking one last sniff, I stepped out of the bathroom and into the bedroom to join Carly.

She'd sunk lower into the pillows, her eyelids half-closed. "You tired?"

"A little."

In the bed beside her, I shoved some pillows behind me and faced her. "Not sure if you want to talk about it. If you don't, that okay, but what happened at the pool?"

"I don't mind talking about it." She stared off into space. "I was concentrating, digging deep inside myself, and I...it's hard to explain."

I stroked her arm. "It's okay. Take your time."

"I met resistance, like hitting a solid door. I had to see what was behind it." She squeezed her eyes shut and covered them with her hands. "I forced it open."

My breath caught in my throat as her lifeless image flashed behind my eyes.

"TriCel files—thousands of them bombarding my brain. I couldn't shut it off, control the data. It took over. Everything grew dark. I remember hitting the water, and then nothing."

"Thank God Zack was there. You could have drowned."

"That's the weird part. I don't remember not being able to breathe."

I struggled to find the right words. I didn't want her to think I blamed TriCel, but I did. It could have killed her. Was it a threat now? How would I protect her? "Should we be worried?"

"About TriCel?" A soft headshake accompanied her firm tone. "I don't think so. I think I initiated the shutdown. I just need to master its power, that's all." She gave me a playful nudge and shrugged it off. "I'm not worried, and you shouldn't be, either."

"I am worried, Carly. It put you in danger tonight. What if it does it again and does something worse?"

"It won't." She sounded so certain.

My arm encircled her, and I pulled her close to me. I had to trust her.

She snuggled up against me and asked, "Are you attracted to me?" Her gaze drifted away.

"That's a silly question. You look like—"

"Not because I look like Jenna. Are you attracted to me?" She pointed at herself.

I studied her expression. "Why do you ask?"

"You've not tried to." She paused. "You haven't shown affection."

I laughed. "Are you talking about sex?"

She nudged me. "It's not funny."

Her words caught me off guard. My brain went blank as if it suddenly stopped working. She knew nothing of intimacy, the surge of uncontrollable emotions that tug at the heart and fuck with the head. Right now we were in the middle of some crazy shit. I didn't have time to think beyond that.

"I'm not saying we should have sex." She shrugged and sighed. "I just want to know if one day."

I softly kissed her lips. "I'm in awe of you, Carly. You take my breath away. One day sounds perfect."

Her eyes sparkled as they searched mine. She squeezed me tight and whispered in my ear, "Thank you."

Chapter 14

My eyelids slowly opened to the sound of water drumming against the tile floor. Carly's side of the bed was empty, and the bathroom door stood ajar. My mind drew the connection. With her in the shower, my body refused to rise as I stretched my arms overhead and yawned.

A knock at the door interrupted my laziness and forced me out of bed to answer it. A woman with grayish hair, dressed in a pale green uniform, stood just shy of the door, neatly folded clothes resting on her arms.

"Yes?"

"Your freshly laundered clothes, Mr. Dillon."

No one called me Mr. Dillon. That was my dad, not me. "Thank you."

"Mrs. Bykov asked me to let you know breakfast would be served in the dining room in a half-hour." With that, she hurried off down the hall.

My smile grew wide as I looked down at our clothes before closing the door. Being waited on hand and foot had its perks. I could totally get used to this lifestyle. "Carly." I tapped on the bathroom door. "They brought our clothes."

The water shut off. "Hang on a minute." She pulled the door all the way open. Her damp hair hung down the middle of her back, and a large towel hugged her body, beads of water dotting her shoulders. "Come in."

I set her clothes on the corner of the vanity. "Good morning."

Her smile reached her eyes. "Morning."

"Breakfast is in a half-hour in the dining room."

"Give me five minutes, then the shower's all yours."

"You got it." I closed the door, about to claim those five minutes in bed when my cell went off. Looked at the number as I grabbed it from the night stand. "Shit. Give it a rest, guys." The FBI had called so many times, I knew the number by sight. They could go to voicemail. Shower, breakfast, and then I'd deal with them.

"Shower's yours."

"That was the shortest five minutes ever."

She flopped down on one of the chairs, still towel-drying her hair. "I'm hungry, so don't take too long."

After grabbing my clothes, I smirked, then shut myself inside the warm bathroom. Setting the temperature, I stepped under the spray and shampooed my hair but axed the shave. Finished my shower in about ten, dressed, and ran the towel through my hair a second time. As I gave a nod to my appearance in the mirror, my stomach growled out a complaint. Now I couldn't get food off my mind. I blamed Carly and her "I'm hungry" comment.

As I stepped out of the bathroom, Carly jumped to her feet. "Let's go eat."

We were the first to arrive. The buffet spread was insane. My brain couldn't decide where to start. Carly dove straight into the eggs. I poured a large cup of coffee, then grabbed some eggs and bacon.

I pulled out a chair for Carly. "Can I get you a coffee or OJ?"

"Coffee, please."

"You got it." My cell went off again—FBI. Ignoring their call, I shoved my phone back into my pocket and poured Carly's coffee.

Alicia entered, dressed in a dark suit, her hair pulled back into her customary ponytail. "Good morning," she greeted, her tone bright and cheery.

"Morning," Carly said before a forkful of eggs entered her mouth.

I held up a mug. "Coffee, Alicia?"

"Black, please. Thank you, Jeremy."

I set Carly's coffee in front of her and Alicia's on the other side of the table. I bit into a piece of bacon and sat back in my seat.

Alicia filled her plate and took a seat opposite Carly and me.

Loud, high-pitched voices and feet pounded against the tile floor. A girl and a boy burst into the dining room, pushing and shoving each other. Their curly blonde hair—hers long and his short—had me thinking they were twins. She pranced around the buffet clad in cutoff shorts and a polka dot crop top. He darted in front of her, sporting cargo shorts and a graphic tee. "I'm first," he teased as he held her back.

"Get out of my way, Luka."

A tall blonde-haired woman clothed in an oversized T-shirt and leggings shouted, "Mila, Luka, that's enough!"

"Good morning, Anya," Alicia calmly greeted as she raised her cup. "Coffee?"

"Do I ever," she said, heading straight for the coffee station.

Alicia made the introductions. "Carly, Jeremy, this is Anya, Vsevolod's sister, and these kiddos are Mila and Luka. Anya, Mila, and Luka, these are our house guests, Carly and Jeremy."

Mila curtsied, and Luka took a bow before waving. "Hi, new people," Luka said.

"Hey," I said, waving back. "Nice to meet everyone."

"You as well," Anya replied, pouring a large cup of coffee and grabbing a banana nut muffin.

Carly sat back in her seat, a look of horror creasing her brow. Teenagers seemed to be something new for her. Getting herself in check, she produced a forced wave.

Mila and Luka claimed chairs on either side of their mother and dived into their breakfast.

Yet again, my cell rang, and again I ignored it. Probably the damn FBI. Out of the corner of my eye, I caught Carly glancing at me. I kept my gaze on my plate and stuffed a forkful of eggs into my mouth. I wanted to finish breakfast before the FBI monopolized the conversation, but I didn't get but two more bites of eggs before my cell sounded off.

Mila snickered. "Someone's popular."

The heat of Carly's gaze burned into me, then she nudged me. "Who keeps calling you?"

I shrugged. "Don't know."

"Jeremy?"

I knew the minute I faced her, she'd know, and the peaceful meal would end. Slowly, I turned to her and our eyes met.

"Are you kidding me? Really, again?"

"It's okay. Let's just finish our breakfast."

She shoved her plate away and sighed deeply. "I lost my appetite. It's never going to end."

The kids grew quiet, their eyes large and on Carly.

Alicia turned her attention toward Carly. "What is it?"

Her cheeks turned red as she shook her head, then stormed out of the room.

I rose to my feet, gave an apologetic, "Excuse me," and rushed after her.

She'd trekked halfway to the stairs before I caught up to her. "Hold on."

She whipped around and faced me, her arms stubbornly crossed over her chest, her shoe tapping the marble tile. "No, I'm sick of this. This ends today!"

Her dead serious expression quickened my pulse. Was I over analyzing her demeanor? I didn't think so. And, more importantly, what did "This ends today" mean? Should I defuse the situation? A virtual nod popped into my head. "I haven't listened to their voicemails. Maybe it's about something else?"

She bobbed her chin toward my pocket. "So listen."

"Okay, hang on." I viewed my voicemails. "There are three."

"Can you put it on speaker?"

Probably wasn't the best idea, especially in her state of mind, but I did it anyway and tapped voicemail number one.

"Jeremy, it's Special Agent Green. We need you and Carly to come to headquarters as soon as possible. We need Carly to identify documents we've uncovered."

She threw up her hands. "I don't need to hear the rest." She brushed my shoulder as she turned back around and stomped toward the front door. "Let's go."

I hesitated. She wasn't thinking straight. Her anger was controlling her. "You sure? Maybe we should get Alicia."

"Now, Jeremy!"

I broke out into a run after her, then skidded to a stop. "My keys are in the bedroom."

"I'll wait by the car."

I took the stairs two at a time, sprinted down the hall, and barged through the bedroom door. My gaze darted about, spotting my keys on the dresser. With keys in hand, I flew down the stairs, catching sight of Alicia standing at the foot of the stairs, her hands on her hips.

"What's going on?"

"Carly's pissed. The FBI wants us at headquarters." I kept a brisk pace as I gave Alicia the 411. "We're heading there now."

Grabbing my arm, she brought me to a standstill. "If you need us, don't hesitate to call."

As I ran toward the door, I shouted over my shoulder, "Thanks, Alicia!"

Carly leaned against the passenger side door, arms crossed, eyes narrowed into slits, looking all badass. I certainly wouldn't mess with her. As I hit the remote, she hopped in before I could get her door for her. I slid into the driver's seat, second-guessing whether to engage in conversation. She'd either welcome it or bite my head off. I was fairly certain it was the latter, but I gave it a shot. "Wonder what documents they're talking about."

She huffed.

So no talking it was.

Her pinched lips and clamped jaw remained the entire way. Uncomfortable silence swelled around us until I pulled into the FBI parking lot and claimed a space up front. Before I'd turned off the engine, she bolted. I trucked after her and latched onto her arm, bringing her asinine mission to a halt. My grip on her shoulders forced her to face me. "You're pissed, I get it. Turn down the volume. Take a breath."

Her glared hardened.

"You go in, guns blazing…" I blinked. "Geez, I sound like my dad." I ditched the awkward thought. "Anyway, they'll home in on your emotions and take advantage. You'll make a mistake."

She balled her fists and shook them at me. "Don't tell me how to act or what to feel. I'm done." She jutted a finger at the building. "No. They're done."

The whole FBI thing had messed with her head. She needed a distraction. I kissed her, caressing her tongue with mine. She stood motionless, her arms slack at her sides, and then she gasped. Relaxing, she leaned into me, her arms wrapping tight around my neck to pull me closer. An electrical jolt awakened my curiosity and my body. I kissed her until the need to breathe pulled us apart. "Feel better?"

She twisted a strand of hair around her finger and giggled. "Yes."

"We'll go in, stand our ground, and then—"

"Go home," she finished for me.

"Agreed. And *our* home, not Vsevolod's."

She gave me a side hug. "I love that you said *our* home."

"Well, of course, it is."

Resting her head on my shoulder for a brief moment, she took a deep breath and blew it out slowly. "I'm ready."

The glass doors slid open as we approached. I entwined our fingers, a small gesture of my affection and support, letting her know I was right there with her. She tightened her grip the minute we stood before the bulletproof box. The officer inside glanced up at us, nodded, then picked up the phone. "Special Agent Green, they're here."

Damn, this stranger knew who we were. A Big Brother moment drew me to peek over my shoulder.

"Please proceed to the security scanners," she advised, waving us forward. "An officer will meet you on the other side."

Once again, we passed underneath the metal frame and into the heart of the FBI. A female officer—clad in dark blue, red hair pulled tight into a bun—waved us forward. "Follow me, please."

She wasted no time escorting us into a room. "Wait here. The agents will be with you shortly."

I turned in a circle. Same table, same chairs, same glass wall. It couldn't possibly be the same room as before, but it felt like déjà vu all over again. The whoosh of the door turned my head. Green and Finch entered, claiming opposite ends of the table, a vanilla folder peeking out from underneath Green's arm. Carly and I sat down together, and once more, I held her hand, giving it a gentle squeeze.

Green set the folder on the table and flipped it open, spreading out several images of people standing inside a cave with mounds of dirt separated into piles, strange symbols carved into the cave wall, and broken artifacts pulled from the dirt piles. Green tapped his finger over the symbols. "Do you recognize these?"

Carly stiffened and let go of my hand. Her jaw clenched as her fingers glided over the glossy film.

I laid my hand on her shoulder. "Carly?"

In a low, barely audible tone, words came rushing out of her mouth, "We are the sun, the moon, the stars. We are all things. We are your creators."

Finch spoke up, his tone elated. "Is that the translation?"

Her head jerked in my direction, her blue eyes mutating into computerized discs. With incredible speed and strength, she yanked my chair next to her. "Do not leave my side."

My eyebrows furrowed as I tried to understand what had happened. With one arm, she'd hauled me and the chair like I weighed nothing. How was that possible?

Green lunged forward, his hand reaching for his gun. Carly's gleaming orbs rotated and locked, her targets Green and Finch. A gasp flew out of Green's mouth as he smashed his hands over his ears. His legs gave out beneath him, and he sagged to the floor. Finch stumbled into the wall, a gargled scream cut short as he collapsed, his cheek slapping against the tile.

Goosebumps slid along the back of my neck as I fixated on their motionless bodies. Were they dead? I reached for Carly's arm, but a muffled shout stopped my hand midair. I cocked my head, listening. A dead calm echoed in my ears. Had I imagined it? A high-pitched shriek suddenly jarred my brain, then another, and another. Hysteria erupted outside the four walls surrounding us. People screamed, the soles of their shoes clobbering the tile, and every few seconds, an eerily loud thud.

I froze. Things were moving too fast to process. What the fuck was going on?

The stench of burnt rubber seeped under the doorframe, burning my eyes. The building shook, cracking the ceiling overhead and hurling a panel to the floor. Live wires dangled from the hole, popping and hissing as they came into contact. My own scream filled my ears, and I flung my arms over Carly, shielding her. Was it a fire? A cyber-attack? Terrorists? My brain calculated another option—Carly. A sudden cold sensation hit my core. I pulled away, looking her over. She sat perfectly still, hands on the table, fingers splayed, and a stream of dark red blood oozing from one of her nostrils.

"Carly." Her demeanor didn't change. I cupped her face in my hands and raised my voice. "Carly!" Her eyes—if you could call them eyes—continued to look forward, a brilliant glow spinning clockwise inside of them. I snapped my fingers in front of her face. The building shuddered, sliding our chairs apart. Metal screeched, and explosions came from all sides, propelling ceiling panels to the floor. Adrenaline shot me to my feet. "We gotta go."

The blue color of Carly's eyes returned before a lifeless and vacant stare took control of them. Her rosy, pink skin mutated into a sickening pasty white as she flopped forward in the chair. "No!" My heartbeat raced as I gently tapped her cheeks, calling her name. She was out cold, the blood now dripping from both nostrils and smearing red streaks across her chin.

My body shook uncontrollably as I grabbed onto her, hoisting her up and into my arms. I flung the door open and staggered backward, a girlish squeal flying out of my mouth. Bodies littered the hallway, legs and arms sprawled, some piled on top of each other. Every computer dangled from the wall, melted, cracked, and broken pieces scattered about the floor. I couldn't move, couldn't think, my eyes raking over the unnerving and chaotic sight. Save Carly, shattering the paralyzing hold.

Stepping into the hall, I zigzagged through the maze of bodies, listening to my own pulse throb in my throat. Were they dead? I had to know. Shifting Carly in my arms, I reached down and pressed my fingertip to one of the officer's necks. A steady thump tapped against my skin. I blurted out, "Thank God," before checking another, then another. All were breathing and with strong pulses. For a moment, I just stared. How could this have happened? I needed answers. Then I looked down at Carly, limp in my arms. This wasn't her normal blackout. She looked...dead. Answers no longer mattered and finding help did.

As I neared the walkthrough scanner, I paused, eyeing the fractured frame and the frayed hanging wires. No sparks or hisses met my ears. The thing appeared destroyed and lifeless. Still, I ran through it, not wanting to take any chance with Carly in my arms. My gaze caught sight of the bulletproof box—not so indestructible anymore. One side was completely gone, flattened to the ground. The glass scattered across the tile and glimmered under the blinking fluorescent lights.

My stomach dropped, and I grasped onto Carly as a screech of metal shattered the silence. I whirled toward the sound, and my gaze fell upon the automatic sliding doors. As they attempted to close, a bent piece of steel wedged between them blocked the motion. The sight of the parking lot through the broken glass propelled me through the turnstiles and away from this nightmare.

A cool breeze chased me as I raced across the pavement, straight for my Explorer. Relentlessly, I clicked the damn remote until the pop of the lock chirped. With one hand, I flung open the passenger side door and set Carly inside, my shaky, clammy hands fumbling with her seatbelt. After three tries, it finally latched. I gasped with relief as I scurried to the driver's side and threw the door open, the edge nailing my thigh. Sharp pain blasted through my leg as I jumped behind the wheel. My lungs deflated, and I gasped for air before growling in frustration and punching the start button.

As I screeched out of the parking lot, I glared at the navigation screen, pounding the steering wheel and screaming, "Come on!" The second the Bluetooth connected, I tapped the voice button.

"Please say a command after the beep."

"Call."

"Say the name you want to call."

I swallowed the lump in my throat and forced out, "Alicia."

"Calling Alicia."

On the fourth ring, I hit the end and immediately called back.

"You've reached Alicia. I'm sorry, I can't take—"

I slammed my palm against the dashboard. "Shit. Answer your damn phone, Alicia!"

A call came in—Alicia's. I tapped accept. "Alicia!"

"Jeremy. Sorry, I was on a call and—"

"Carly's injured." My voice cracked. "There's blood. I don't know what to do."

"What happened?"

"We were at FBI headquarters. There were bodies everywhere, and Carly blacked out!"

"Calm down. What do you mean, bodies?"

"At the FBI!" I shouted at the screen. "I don't have time. Carly needs help!" I looked over at her. "Blood is coming from her nose. I'm driving her to the hospital."

"No," she barked out. "Bring her to The Dollmaker."

"Alicia, you don't understand. She needs a doctor."

"Jeremy, she's not human. She needs our team of scientists. How fast can you get her here?"

"Fifteen minutes, maybe."

"I'll meet you in the lobby."

I was going in the opposite direction. Taking the far-left lane, I made a sharp U-turn and headed for The Dollmaker. The rise and fall of Carly's chest encouraged me, but I needed more and reached over and squeezed her hand—her warm flesh was equally encouraging. But her skin was so pale, and the blood...why the blood? For a brief second, I took my eyes off the road and looked heavenward. "Please, God, let her be okay."

Chapter 15

Arriving at The Dollmaker, I parked at an angle, taking up two spots. Rays of sunlight stretched over the building, shining in my eyes as I scooped up Carly's lifeless body into my arms and ran toward the entrance. Alicia was already there waiting with the door opened, waving me inside where five people—three males, two females—wearing white lab coats surrounded her. I didn't get a foot past the threshold before the team of five hijacked Carly and wheeled her away on a gurney loaded with medical supplies, their destination the elevators.

"I'm coming with her!" I shouted, hopping inside just before the doors closed.

As the elevator hummed and thrust upward, Alicia turned to me, her hands on her hips. "What the hell happened?"

I swiped at my eyes, attempting to stop the tears that threatened to fall. "I don't know. We were just sitting there, then things went batshit crazy."

"Details, Jeremy."

"Bodies scattered across the floor," I blurted out. "Computers melted. The building just fell apart." I lowered my voice and confessed, "I think Carly did it."

A look of disbelief spread across Alicia's face.

The five people hovering over Carly, hooking her up to monitors and jabbing her veins with IV needles, hadn't given my words the slightest bit of attention. My gaze followed the IV line to the clear bag of fluid hooked to the gurney. "Is she going to be okay?"

The tallest man, with short gray hair speckled with white, looked at me over his metal-framed glasses sitting low on his nose. "We're going to do everything we can."

My mouth went dry. That wasn't the guarantee I was looking for. My gaze shifted to Alicia, pleading for help.

She raised her hand in a calming gesture before turning toward the man. "Dr. Kane, what are you thinking?"

"We need diagnostics and a head CT scan. We'll need to run a series of tests before I know anything."

"Carly's favorite thing," I breathed out.

The elevator took us to the fifth floor. The team of five ushered Carly into the hallway, each carrying a device attached to her. The wheels of the gurney clattered against the tile as they rushed toward a pair of double doors at the end of the hallway to a restricted area. I shrugged it off. I was the purchaser, so of course, they'd let me in.

Alicia caught my arm and pulled me back. "This is as far as we go."

I jerked my arm away. "No, I'm going with her."

Alicia nodded to the man she'd called Dr. Kane. Tapping his badge against a scanner on the left side, the doors whooshed apart, and they quickly ducked inside with Carly. I charged forward, but not fast enough. An automated locking mechanism clicked, securing the doors and shutting me out. I tried pulling on the handle, but the damn thing wouldn't budge. Gripping the metal knob with both hands, I groaned, yanking as hard as I could, but got nothing. I glared at Alicia over my shoulder. "Open the door!"

"Jeremy, she's in good hands. We just have to wait."

"Alicia, open the damn door, now!"

"There's nothing you can do for her. They need to do their jobs, and you need to let them."

I punched my fist into the door and screamed, "Open the fucking door!" As tears streamed down my cheeks, I kicked its frame, crying, "Carly!'"

Alicia tucked her arm beneath mine and gently turned me away from the doors. "There's a room just down the hall where we can wait."

I slung my arm around her shoulders and slumped against her. My chin trembled as I mumbled, "I can't let anything happen to her."

"She's in the best of hands." Her tone rang with truth.

I bobbed my head in acknowledgment, surrendered, and let her lead me away like a hunched-over old man who'd lost his way.

"Here we are." She opened the door and guided me inside.

The room gave off a staff lounge vibe. It had a small kitchenette with a mini-fridge in the corner and a circular table with four chairs tucked underneath. On the opposite side, an L-shaped sectional claimed one wall with two oversized chairs facing the sectional. A coffee table sat between them, and a large TV hung on the wall across from the seating area.

I plopped down into an oversized chair, cradled my head in my hands, and let out an exaggerated groan. Tears fell onto my jeans, and my nose wouldn't stop running.

Alicia set a box of Kleenex next to me, then headed into the kitchenette. "The strongest we have is beer."

I grabbed a handful of Kleenex. "Beer works."

Returning with two bottles, she handed me one. I chugged the bitter ale, letting it moisten my dry throat. Setting the half-empty bottle on the coffee table, I eyed it, considering finishing it whole.

What the hell? I downed the rest in a single gulp. Alicia passed me the second beer, and I took a few sips. "Thank you."

"Ready to tell me what really happened?"

"Yeah, I think so." I settled back in the chair, took another sip of beer, and closed my eyes. "It all happened so fast. We were in the room, and they showed us these pictures. Carly said something about the moon and the stars, then she changed, got really quiet. And her eyes, you know..." I couldn't finish.

"The computer eyes?" Alicia asked, yet nodded as if she already knew.

"She directed some kind of power through them. Green and Finch went down, and there was all this noise. People were screaming and running. The ceiling collapsed, and that's when I saw the blood running out of Carly's nose. I tried to reach her, but she just sat there, staring with those computerized eyes."

"You mentioned bodies. Dead bodies?"

Stepping over their lifeless forms flashed behind my eyes. That tense stomach, the breath that catches in your throat, threatened to return. The feelings Alicia was probably struggling with now. "No, thank God. They were breathing, had pulses. Just out cold, like they were drugged."

"Drugged?"

"I don't know, Alicia. The entire FBI was fine one minute, and the next, they were dropping like flies, and the computers looked..." I paused, searching for the right word. "Melted or fried."

"Are you sure it wasn't some kind of an attack camouflaged by what Carly attempted?"

I looked her directly in the eyes and mimicked my dad's firm, authoritative tone. "Wouldn't the FBI be prepared for that? This was Carly. Things went haywire after her eyes mutated, and she told me not to leave her side," I pointed out. "I think she protected me, kept me safe. Otherwise, I would've collapsed."

A knock at the door got my attention. Words stuck in my throat. All that mattered was who was on the other side of that door.

Dr. Kane entered, his lips pressed into a thin line, his hands clasped in front of him.

Alicia rose, her hand reaching and wrapping around her throat. "Dr. Kane?"

"I have an update," his voice softspoken. "The scan showed brain swelling. There's a small bleed, but her body will absorb that. These are all normal reactions to injury."

If that was normal, why the somber expression?

"We'll have to wait for the swelling to go down before we know the extent of the damage, if any."

I blinked. What did that mean? Why would he say that? Aren't doctors supposed to state the positive? "Damage?"

"Currently, she has very little brain activity. This may increase as the swelling goes down or it may not. We just don't know yet."

"And if it doesn't?"

He paused; a grave expression washed over his face. "She may never wake up."

I flinched. Time slowed as my thoughts raced backward, dredging up the nightmare of Jenna's death. That monotone voice on the other end of the phone, "There's been an accident…" I jabbed my fingers into my temples, pushing the memory from my head. I couldn't, wouldn't, let it happen again. "Carly wouldn't do that to me," I blurted, clenching my fists. "She just wouldn't. She'll wake up."

Alicia's voice lost confidence as she asked, "When will you know more?"

"We should have a better idea by morning."

Pushing to my feet, I eyed the door. My place was by Carly's bedside, not sitting in this room drinking beer to numb my pain. "Can I be with her? She needs to hear my voice."

He gave an understanding nod. "Of course. I'll take you to her."

He led Alicia and me to a different part of the building. The Dollmaker's futuristic décor was gone, replaced by sterile white walls, lackluster tile, and that smell of disinfectant. Machines broadcasting an annoying beep, lab supplies stocked on shelves, and empty gurneys cluttered the hallway. Was this their version of a hospital? A hospital for broken dolls? On the opposite side of the hall stood several closed doors with numbers painted above their frames. Dr. Kane stopped at number three. "Stay as long as you like. I'll be back later to check on her."

I stood motionless at the door. Alicia opened it for me and guided me inside. Carly lay tucked into a hospital bed, an IV drip hanging overhead, and a monitor displaying colorful stats at her bedside. Her skin reclaimed its rosy-pink hue, and I sagged against Alicia. "Her color's back. That's a good sign, right?"

Alicia pulled me into a side hug. "I think it is."

I leaned over Carly and kissed her forehead before pulling a chair close to her and taking her hand in mine. "I'm here, Carly."

Alicia rested her hand on my shoulder and said, "I'm going to go call Vsevolod."

I didn't take my gaze off Carly as I nodded. "Okay."

She closed the door, leaving me alone with Carly. I brought her hand to my lips and kissed it, then rubbed it against my cheek.

"Don't leave me, Carly," I whispered. "You're strong, a fighter. You've got this. Please come back to me."

I received no reaction or reply from her. A thickness spread down my throat, threatening more tears. I didn't know how to help, but talking to her, touching her, and letting her hear my voice all felt right. Somewhere deep inside her, I believed she heard every word I said, felt my touch, and knew I was at her bedside.

The whoosh of the door sounded behind me. Alicia came around to the opposite side and sank onto the bench next to the window, her eyebrows bunched, her mouth pinched. I was certain I wore that same expression. How had things spiraled so far out of control? And how would I reclaim the normalcy for Carly and me? I couldn't think about that. I had to focus on the now. One thing at a time. "I can't go home. Can I stay here with her?"

She didn't even hesitate. "Of course. Vsevolod and I will stay here as well. He's on his way."

"Thank you. And the doctors? They'll stay too?"

"Oh, yes, absolutely. Patients come first." She glanced around the room. "Let me see about getting an extra cot for you."

"I won't be able to sleep." I smoothed Carly's hair. "She should've woken up by now."

"This blackout is…"

"Way worse," I finished for her. "Her brain's fried." A sob strangled my words.

"We don't know that."

Tears rolled down my cheeks as my shoulders trembled. "She has to be okay."

Alicia's arms wrapped around me, and I clung to her, my chest heaving with uncontrollable sobs. I couldn't tell Matt or Missy, my parents, or Mr. Clean. They'd want to be with me, to comfort me, but they wouldn't understand her being at The Dollmaker and not a hospital. Alicia and Vsevolod knew the truth. I could confide in them, gather their support, lean on them. They were all I had.

It seemed like forever before I let go. My eyes ached, and my nose was running. "Excuse me, Alicia." I went into the bathroom and blew the hell out of my nose, washed my face, then stared at my puffy, red, pain-stricken expression. I looked like shit. Falling apart wasn't going to help anyone, especially Carly. As I filled my lungs, I held onto the calming breath before blowing it out and returning to the room.

Alicia offered me a sad smile.

"I'm okay. I just needed a moment."

"No need to explain. Totally understand. I'm going to see about getting that cot." She held up a hand before I could object. "I know, I know, but even if you can't sleep, you may want to lie down and rest for a bit. Are you hungry? I can have my staff place an order and have it delivered."

"I'm not hungry, but thanks."

"Maybe later." She tapped her cell and requested, "Call Greg."

"Mrs. Bykov, what can I do for you?" he replied in a bright and cheery voice.

"Greg, can you please bring a cot with some extra pillows and blankets to room three?"

"You got it."

"Thank you, Greg." After putting down her phone, she raked her hand through her hair and scanned the room.

"Are you scared too?"

Her gaze came to a sudden stop and focused on me. Her expression softened. "Maybe a bit anxious. I just feel so helpless."

"I appreciate you being here. Handling this alone, I don't think I could do it."

She lowered herself onto the bench, her gaze settling on Carly. "Her color looks much better."

I sat upright and offered a crisp nod. "I thought so too. That's a good sign, right?"

"I think so."

A knock came as the door slowly opened. A woman entered, a white lab coat covering her clothes and her auburn hair piled into a bun. "Hello, I'm Emily. I'll be taking Carly's vitals throughout the night."

"I'm Jeremy," I said, scooting my chair back and giving her room.

Alicia gave a nod. "Hi, Emily."

"Hello, Mrs. Bykov."

Carly didn't stir as Emily checked her blood pressure, temperature, and flashed a penlight in her eyes. After typing on her tablet, Emily looked up and offered a pleasant smile. "Her vitals are all good. I'll be back later to check on her." She stepped out of the room and quietly closed the door behind her.

Another knock immediately followed, and I sighed as Alicia opened the door.

"Good to see you, Mrs. Bykov." An older man with stark white hair and eyebrows to match, clad in a janitor's uniform, wheeled in a cot topped with extra blankets and pillows.

"And you, Greg." Alicia gestured to the corner of the room. "You can put it there."

"Sure thing. You need anything else, you just let me know."

"Thank you."

Once again, the door closed and we were alone. I waited a good minute before settling into the chair next to Carly, giving her hand a reassuring squeeze. "I'm not going anywhere." Her hand lay limp inside mine. I'd hoped for a twitch of a finger, a soft squeeze back, or any movement, no matter how small, to let me know she knew I was there. A willingness to do anything to help fluttered inside my chest. If only I knew what that was.

****

Close to an hour and a half later, Vsevolod walked into the room. "What took you so long?" Alicia asked.

He looked at me before letting his gaze linger on Carly. After a few moments, he looked away and focused on us. "I went to the FBI headquarters."

Alicia gasped. "Why?"

"You said bodies," he stated as if that was answer enough. "How could I not investigate in case we needed to lawyer up?"

I scooted to the edge of the chair, staring him down. "What did you see?"

"Well, no bodies."

My head snapped back. How the hell was that possible? A thought occurred—maybe they all woke up.

"We've had quite the time here, Vsevolod," Alicia murmured, her voice shaky. "I'm not in the mood to guess, so just tell us."

He pushed his hands in a downward motion. "Relax. Give me a chance to."

She waited, but he just stared at her.

Finally, he said, "The place was a mess. There was broken glass, ceilings caved in, and destroyed computers. Green walked right past and didn't recognize me. I stood there and gawked at his backside." Vsevolod looked back to Carly. "What did our girl do?"

Chapter 16

I woke with a start and scrambled off the cot with no recollection of dozing off. My gaze darted to Carly, but there was no change. Alicia and Vsevolod weren't in the room. What time was it? I grabbed my cell—5:15 a.m. Before settling into the chair, I scrubbed my face and shook off the daze. "Good morning." I leaned over and kissed her lips, letting mine linger on hers. "Please give me a sign today, Carly."

My stomach rumbled in protest, in need of food. Having not eaten anything since yesterday at breakfast, I decided I would be taking Alicia up on that offer. *Gonna be another long day.*

A gentle tap at the door drew my gaze away from Carly, and I watched as Emily entered.

"More vitals?"

"She's scheduled for her second head CT." Emily capped off Carly's IV and then reached under the bed and pulled a lever.

"Oh, okay. So this scan will tell us if the swelling's decreased?"

She maneuvered the bed away from the wall and rolled it toward the door. "Dr. Kane will discuss everything with you." She offered a sympathetic smile like she knew something I didn't, which was probably true. "I'll bring her back shortly."

I wasn't going to get any details out of her. As I watched her wheel Carly down the hallway, my stomach twisted into a knot. Where the hell was Alicia? I needed reassurance, someone to calm my nerves, to tell me everything would be okay. My eyes closed, and I covered them with my hands. "Please let the news be good," I said out loud as I slumped into the chair.

Every few minutes, I checked my cell for the time. How long did a scan take? She'd said "shortly." It had been twenty-five minutes. What equaled shortly? I tilted my ear toward the open doorway, listening for the rub of wheels on the tile, but it was quiet. I popped out of the chair and peeked into the hall, looking right then left, but the corridor was empty.

Five more minutes passed. Cold, clammy sweat coated my palms as worst-case scenarios tortured my mind: the swelling magnified, they found a tumor, she flatlined on the table. I couldn't sit still and paced around the room, counting the seconds in my head.

Wheels clattering against the tile sent an electric jolt scurrying down my spine. I bolted into the hallway and spotted Emily wheeling Carly toward me.

"I'm so sorry for the delay. Dr. Kane was on a call. We had to wait for him to view the images in case he wanted more views."

"Did the swelling go down?"

"I'm not a doctor, but I did see improvement."

I took a shaky breath. "Thank God."

"Dr. Kane will be by shortly and provide more details." She hooked Carly back up to the IV. "Do you need anything before I go?"

"No, thank you."

She gave me that same sympathetic smile before leaving the room.

Carly looked as though she was sleeping peacefully. *If only that were true.* Once more, I sat and reached for her hand. "Carly, I hope you know I'm here, and that I'm not going anywhere. When you open your eyes, I'll be the first person you see."

My stomach picked that moment to growl. How could I possibly think about food? Though, at some point, I'd have to eat something or I'd pass out.

A soft knock at the door drew my gaze away from Carly. Alicia and Vsevolod walked in carrying brown paper bags and cups of coffee.

My body slumped in the chair as I pressed my palm to my heart. "Thank God you're here. They just brought her back from getting a head CT. Dr. Kane is supposed to be by soon with an update."

"No change?" Vsevolod asked, his voice thicker than usual.

"Emily said the swelling had gone down."

"That's good news, Jeremy," Alicia said, handing me a bag and a cup of coffee.

The delicious smell of eggs, potatoes, and rich coffee drifted under my nose. "I'm starving. Thank you, Alicia."

"I wasn't going to ask this time. You have to take care of yourself to take care of Carly."

A wrinkle etched into Vsevolod's forehead as he rubbed his chin. "What's keeping her from waking?"

"My thoughts exactly," I said.

"If she indeed caused the shutdown of the FBI and erased memories..." He gave his head a good shake. "I can't even comprehend the power needed to accomplish such a task."

"Our diagnostics showed her blackouts were self-induced," Alicia offered up before biting into a breakfast burrito. "Maybe her body sensed AI failure and shut down."

Another knock at the door sent my pulse racing. I pushed my food aside, took a deep breath, and mentally prepared myself for the news, good or bad.

Dr. Kane entered, carrying a tablet. "Good morning. I'm glad you're all here."

Vsevolod sliced his hand through the air and ordered, "Just give it to us straight. No beating around the bush."

"The swelling has reduced dramatically. However, her brain activity has not changed. We should see a higher level at this stage. I'm sorry. I wish I had better news."

I could barely breathe as my heart sank inside my chest. His words couldn't be true. Alicia's arm encircled my shoulders, and I sagged against her.

"Why hasn't her brain function increased?" Vsevolod demanded.

"Unfortunately, I don't know. We're dealing with a synthetic brain, not a human one."

I cringed inside. What was he saying? Because she wasn't human, he couldn't save her?

"What are our options? There must be something you can do because she *is* synthetic."

Dr. Kane exuded calm and focus as he spoke in a lower-pitched tone. "The artificial intelligence brain may no longer be functioning. We can rebuild her brain or…" He paused, his gaze shifting from Vsevolod to Alicia and then to me. "Assemble a new Elite model."

I looked to the floor as my thoughts scrambled to understand. Had I heard him right? Carly wasn't just some object that could be replaced or discarded. She had emotions, thoughts, feelings. He couldn't replace that. He had to fix her. I pushed to my feet. Summoning my most forceful tone, I demanded, "You can't just cut out her brain. You need to heal her."

"I don't know that I can," he stated.

Vsevolod gripped my shoulder, a fatherly expression pulling at his brows. "What Dr. Kane is suggesting might be the only way to save her. She'd still be Carly, just a new version of her."

I pushed him away. "Carly is who she is because of TriCel. You remove her brain, you remove TriCel. She wouldn't be Carly. She'd be a carbon copy of Jenna." I blinked slowly, absorbing my own words, then sank back into the chair. Jenna had been my everything, my reason for living, and the reason I created Carly; however, Carly wasn't Jenna. She wasn't even a human. The flawless skin, perfect eyebrows, and beautiful smile she possessed were all man-made, but one thing I knew for certain was that Carly would never leave me. She'd fight to come back to me. My heart knew it to be true, so I had to fight for her. "She'll come back to me," I said out loud.

"Jeremy, Carly isn't—"

Alicia cut Vsevolod off. "We should wait and give her more time." Her eyes moistened as she looked at me.

Dr. Kane gave an understanding nod. "Very well. We'll keep her on fluids and monitor her vitals." His gaze centered on me. "And you do your part, Jeremy. Talk to her, keep her stimulated. Let her know you're here."

"Already on it."

He offered me a genuine smile before leaving the room.

Vsevolod lowered his head and rubbed the back of his neck. "I don't want to sound pessimistic—"

"Then don't."

Ignoring me, he continued. "You have to prepare yourself that she may never wake up."

With a strong, decisive nod, I assured, "You're wrong." I slammed my palm against my chest, just above my heart. "I feel her here. You have to trust me."

Alicia rested her hand on Vsevolod's arm. "We trust you."

Chapter 17

My sleeping Carly hadn't responded to my touches, voice, tears—nothing. She laid there motionless in a world all her own, and I'd had yet to leave her side. Not for food, a change of clothes, or a shower. Thank God for Alicia. She had her staff order takeout whenever I asked and had given me access to the janitor's locker room. I wasn't sure if it was for her sake or the staff's. I mean, you can only go so many days without showering or a change of clothes. I could grab a quick shower and at least change into a clean janitor's uniform all while staying close to Carly, as I promised her I'd be the first person she saw when she woke up. It was a promise I intended to keep. Nothing else mattered.

Day six was no different. I sat next to her, chomping on a burger, clad in a dull gray janitor's uniform. I had *The Passage* sitting on the side table, ready to read to her after lunch. I took the last bite of my burger, licked my fingers, and sucked down half of my soda. I reached for the book but pulled my hand back and trekked into the bathroom to wash off the grease.

Drying them with a towel, I stood in the doorway, looking out the window. Sunlight poured in, spreading beams of light across the room. "What a beautiful day," I murmured.

"Why are you wearing a janitor's uniform?"

"Because I don't want to leave—" I froze as Carly's sweet voice caressed my ears. I dropped the towel and went still. Was I hearing things now? Turning, I gazed into Carly's eyes.

She sat upright, her flawless, beautiful face smiling at me. A bark of laughter flew out of my mouth as I jumped on the bed and kissed her lips over and over again, tears welling up in my eyes. "I knew you wouldn't leave me."

A giggle flowed past her lips as she threw her arms around me. "Did you miss me?"

I laid alongside her and gave her a playful nudge. "Are you kidding me? You scared the shit out of me, Carly. What the hell happened?"

She studied a single spot on the wall for a minute or two before looking back at me. "I couldn't control the power, like at Vsevolod's. My brain lit up like fireworks. The sting of it popping against my skull and my body collapsing, I knew I had only seconds to survive, if that. Complete shutdown was the only way to escape the irreversible fatal error I knew was coming."

"I was scared shitless," I repeated, my stomach clenching. "Watching you lying there, motionless. I felt so helpless."

She became quiet, her lips twisting into a snarl. "That picture."

"The symbols?"

"Yes. It awakened something inside of me—something ancient and powerful."

I pulled away, taking in her expression. "Am I about to hear what TriCel is?"

Her eyes searched mine, shifting back and forth. "If I tell you, no joking. I'm serious."

"You can't not tell me. I mean, come on. I'm just as much a part of this as you, but I promise,"—I crossed my heart—"no joking."

She deliberately lowered her head and stared, assessing my sincerity. Seeming satisfied, she explained, "TriCel did come from Earth, but not Earth as you know it. It's a parallel universe, camouflaged behind it."

Angling my body away from her, I frowned. "Impossible."

"Jeremy."

"What? That wasn't a joke. Parallel universes? Come on. Scientists would've been all over that. We'd already know about something so significant."

"The dense atmosphere hides it from the human eye."

So what, there's like, Earth one and Earth two? My lips twitched, a grin struggling to form, but I tensed my jaw to hide my amusement. I'd promised no joking, no matter how farfetched her story. Besides, I'd experienced more than my fair share of weird shit lately, so what was a little more? She deserved the courtesy of me hearing her out. "So TriCel came from this other universe?"

"Yes. And it's not artificial intelligence. It's the core of a brain's central power."

"What?" I blurted out. "Whose brain?"

"Just listen."

"But—"

"Jeremy."

I pressed my lips together and gestured locking them and tossing away the imagery key.

"Good. Now, that scientist who found TriCel at the excavation site shouldn't have. It was never supposed to have been uncovered. Every so often, a ripple occurs in the fiber of the parallel universe, much like an earthquake."

"TriCel fell through to Earth? *Our* Earth?"

"And was found by the scientist."

"This parallel universe...have you seen it?"

"More like, felt." Her gaze flicked upward as she tapped a finger to her chin. "And not the universe, them. The Alku. They saved me, healing the damage I'd caused."

A slight chill crept over my skin. *Alku?* I pulled away, my eyes searching hers. "Are you still…you?"

She squeezed my hand and assured, "It's okay. I'm still me."

"I don't understand."

"My obsession with stopping the FBI…you were right, I screwed up. I came in too hot. My injuries were far more destructive than at the pool." Tears welled in her eyes. "But I couldn't leave you."

I pressed her hand against my chest. She shuddered out a few shaky breaths before her body relaxed against mine.

"I remember light—warm-like sunshine flooding my body. Alku light, not TriCel, healing the gashes, the contusions, the swelling—all the damage I'd caused. They surrounded me every day, feeding me their lifeforce and bringing me back to you."

I searched her eyes, looking for any subtle changes—a shade of deeper blue, larger pupils, an inhumane sheen, but there was nothing. She was just Carly. I kissed her hand and then her lips. "You're really you."

Her soft laughter tickled my ear. "Yes."

"And the FBI?"

Tension gripped her jaw, her expression instantly altered. "Their constant probing into our lives was never going to stop."

I nodded. That was something we could both agree on.

"The symbols roused TriCel and the Alku." Her brows bunched together. "I'm not sure how to describe it. It's like preternatural strength transforming my body. At that moment, I knew I possessed the Alku power to wipe out everything, such as servers, computers, files." Her lips curled as she made clear, "And purge TriCel from their minds." She brushed the back of her hand down my cheek. "But not you or me. I had to protect us and block the high-pitched frequency that would destroy everything those assholes had on TriCel—me."

"Jesus, Carly." The tips of my fingers rest against my furrowed brow. "I'm having a hard time comprehending all of this. It's just so out there."

"I'm sorry," she murmured, the pain in her voice evident.

"No, no." I hugged her, internally kicking myself. "I didn't mean it like that. It's just...this is beyond my grasp. The parallel universe, Alku, healing light. Are they, like...?" I had no idea how to refer to them. Were they those gem-like globes? Did they have a physical form?

"Like light. That's the only way I know how to explain their appearance," she answered, seeming to know what I was going to ask. "As beings, they're highly intelligent, thoughtful, humane souls sophisticated in technology light-years beyond mankind." She pointed a finger into her chest. "I attacked the FBI—me, not the Alku. It was my decision to use their power." Her tone rose a level as she rushed out, "The FBI's lies, their investigations, wanting control over TriCel, over me, the invasion of our privacy...I had to stop them but still keep them safe."

I pulled her against my shoulder and stroked her hair. "I don't need justification. I'm on your side. They were assholes who deserved everything they got. What amazes me is that a 110-pound doll took down the FBI."

She laughed out loud and squeezed me tight. "I really like you, Jeremy."

"And I really like you, Carly."

We held each other for several minutes before pulling apart. I gazed into her blue eyes and released a sigh. I could stay lost in them forever.

She caressed my cheek and told me, "I heard everything you said, felt your touch. I knew you were by my side the entire time. Thank you for not giving up on me, for believing in me."

I softly kissed her and whispered in her ear, "I will always believe in you. I knew you'd find your way back to me."

A beautiful smile brightened her face. "Of course I would."

I couldn't help but smile back. She'd saved me, brought me back to life, and made me a better person. She'd opened her heart to me, and I loved her for that. "How would you like to go to Florida?"

"Florida?"

"Yeah." My heartbeat drummed inside my chest as I conceded, "To meet my parents."

Her look of shock settled into one of warmth. "I would love to meet your parents."

"But I do have a condition."

"Which is?"

I sliced my hand through the air but couldn't keep a serious tone as lighthearted laughter bled into my voice. "Don't pull that TriCel-Alku shit again."

Grinning, she considered my words. "And what if I need to save the world?"

I sighed dramatically. "I guess I could make an exception...ya know, for the world's sake."

About the Author

LAURA DALEO is the author of six books. She is best known for her storytelling of the vampiric persuasion. Her *Immortal Kiss* series is an interesting twist on the Egyptian pantheon being the original vampires. Her current project, *Once We Were Witches*, is a modern-day, dark fantasy where witchcraft is forbidden. She lives in sunny San Diego, California, with her four dogs, Stuart, Morgan, Dexter, and Rose.

www.ingramcontent.com/pod-product-compliance
Lightning Source LLC
Chambersburg PA
CBHW021333190726
48288CB00003B/1083